I0599639

The Pursuit of Shadows: The Last Warden

Book 1

Edward Kane

Stranded Publications

To my friends,

the ones who aren't here anymore.

Copyright © 2024-2025 by Edward Kane / Stranded Publications

All rights reserved.

No part of this publication may be reproduced, distributed, or transmitted in any form or by any means, including photocopying, recording, or other electronic or mechanical methods, without the prior written permission of the publisher, except as permitted by U.S. copyright law. For permission requests, contact Stranded Publications.

https://www.edwardkane.net/

The story, all names, characters, and incidents portrayed in this production are fictitious. No identification with actual persons (living or deceased), places, buildings, and products is intended or should be inferred.

This book was initially funded via a successful Kickstarter campaign.

Book Cover by 100covers

Illustrations by Stipan Morian

Also by Edward Kane

Available now:

The Redirection of Forever (stories)

The Pursuit of Shadows

The Last Warden

Ruiner – May 2025

The Searing Sentinel – 2025

Contents

THE PURSUIT OF
SHADOWS

Endless

The entire apartment building had been quiet, so much so that when I heard a clatter it made me peek out my front door. That's when I saw it.

There was a briefcase stood up in front of apartment number 10, beside their door mat. It was strange, why not put it on the door mat? The rain was pattering on the roof that morning... Was it Tuesday or Monday? Huh, I'm not sure now.

The next day, it was sunny, and as I exited my apartment I was blinded by a little glare bouncing off the lock on the briefcase. Which was now in front of apartment number 9, where an odd old woman who always smelled of boiled beans and calamine lotion lived. She incorrectly called me Sonny, and I never tried to correct her. I grew to like it more than my own name. Stan was not a fun name; it couldn't be made playful by an addition of a *y* or *ie*.

As my eyes adjusted to the glare, I remembered the skylight above number 10 had been broken months earlier and never repaired. Maybe they'd get to it once number 10 was done being renovated. Who knew when that'd be, as I hadn't seen any sign of maintenance in—uh, again, hard to keep track of time when the same day is seemingly repeated.

When I returned home that evening, the briefcase was nowhere to be seen. I paid it no mind until the next morning; when I saw it again and remembered I hadn't seen it in the afternoon, only the morning. It stood beside the door to apartment number 8 where Tina, the eager divorcee lived. She sometimes waited for me in the morning so she could stand very close to me in the elevator. I had told her several times that she was not the kind of person I was interested in. As of late, I'd wondered if I'd been too subtle with my mention of her having the wrong equipment. No, that wasn't right, because when was the last time I saw her? No matter. I didn't hear any jingling keys so

I was in the clear. Quietly, I passed by her door and the briefcase which seemed to look at me as I passed.

I slipped through the stairway door and heard footfalls below. I peered over the railing and saw a tall man with round sunglasses that barely covered his eyes. What use were those? He heard the door close and looked up at me. Behind the tinted glasses I saw glowing gold textured eyes. Then in a flash, he was gone except for the echoing clatter of dress shoes on metal stairs.

Fear forced me to lean against the railing and it was pain in my left wrist that brought me back to center. I stood up and shook out my wrist. After a deep breath, I swallowed and carefully made my way down the four flights of stairs. The complete silence felt sinister and the layer of dust on the railing seemed unreal. How long had it been since I'd used the stairs? Then again, how often would I have used the railing?

When I made it to the mail room on the bottom floor, I expected to see Gold Eyes there, but there was no one. I realized I'd left my mailbox key upstairs, so

I proceeded around the corner to the double doors leading out to the parking lot.

The smell of dust was replaced with ash and soot. The glass windows of the doors were painted over with off-white paint, and poorly done at that. Maintenance was never great at maintenance, hence the dust and the stained carpets throughout the building. It made me sick, so I tried not to think about it.

I pressed my body against the door handlebar and it didn't budge. There was a faint feeling of something behind me and when I turned, I saw him.

Gold Eyes.

This time his glasses were gone and I saw the full breadth of the two large ovals made entirely of hard gold flakes where his eyes should be. I watched as he held a finger up, and wagged it back and forth.

"You can't go that way," he said in a flat tone that sounded more like a dull hum than words. When he spoke, he left his jaw open as if he had to manually close it, but his fingers were preoccupied.

Then, he turned on his heel and started toward the side door partially hidden in an alcove beside the staircase that was marked: For Official Use Only. He waved at it, and the door burst open.

Before I knew it, I found myself following into the open door. The lock had been broken and there was no way the door would be able to stand back up on its own, as it was a pull and Gold Eyes had pushed it in. So much of the building was in a state of disarray, it was a shock it was still standing.

I wanted to speak but couldn't. Gold Eyes flew through the corridors like he had no time to actually land his feet on the floor. It didn't make any sense.

Running, I barely could take stock of all the junk that littered the hallways. How was this building real? A maintenance hall overflowing as storage. It made my head hurt.

Ahead of us, the hall degraded and the off-white walls grew darker and darker, as if the mold was growing outward from a source deep inside the building. As I moved, I watched the building deteriorate. I felt my feet slow and I swallowed hard, resulting in a cough.

Gold Eyes stopped and faced me.

I halted, my feet slipping on the floor and with them words began spilling out of my mouth, "What about the briefcase?"

He turned his head to one side, and his jaw dropped open. After a beat, words began to flood the hall.

"Your condition is far from brief. You've been here too long."

"What condition? What are you talking about?"

Gold Eyes recoiled. His mouth slammed shut like someone else was in control and he was just a puppet.

"Tell me what's going on. Why wouldn't the door open?"

He shook his head.

"What the fuck is going on!"

He shook his head even harder.

I took a step toward him. I wanted to grab the bastard and shake him. Shake the words out of him. As I reached out, he did too and grabbed my hands, pulling me close to him. My feet slipped out from under me and he cradled me in his arms. His jaw fell open and he leaned down to where I was like he was going to kiss me—instead saliva trickled off his tongue and hit my chin. He recoiled, as if he was testing me. My feet disobeyed, backpedaling me away from him. Then my hand went to brush the saliva away. Immediately, I was surprised by the prickle of facial hair all along my face. I had shaved that morning before work, I was sure of it.

The burning pain from the saliva pulled me away. It was hotter than anything I'd ever touched. I wanted to close my eyes and scream, but I couldn't look away from his face. I couldn't take my eyes away from the strange ovals that were his eyes.

"Unlike you, I am not blind."

I shook my head, trying to convey that I didn't understand.

He snatched me, drew me in close again. He stared at me for a moment then looked away.

His hands let go and I gasped as I fell. I clenched my eyes closed while wondering if I should have said something. When I opened my eyes, I was looking up at my bedroom ceiling. I closed my eyes again and kept them shut for a few seconds before opening them.

Still, my bedroom.

"What the fuck?" I yelled.

I leapt from the bed and bolted for the front door. It nearly came off the hinges when I yanked it open. The building's disarray had made its way to me. I looked around and saw the briefcase beside number 7, two doors from me. I ran out into the hall and scooped up the case. The lock looked broken and the handle barely held on. The thing was in rough shape.

Back inside the apartment, I slammed it down on the kitchen counter and to my surprise it popped open and as it did, I heard glass cracking and falling in the hall. Followed by a huge thud.

The stench of ash and soot filled my nostrils.

I walked away from the briefcase and as I approached the open door a slight breeze hit me and when I looked into the hall, I saw a slender man with broad wings wrapped around him like a blanket. The feathers smelled pleasant like a waft of a distant sandy paradise. I wanted to be in his arms, where I could feel those feathers.

The wings opened and I saw Gold Eyes for what he was—an angel sent to me. His jaw fell open and I saw thousands of teeth like little jagged thunderbolts all lined up and ready to tear my flesh.

I stepped into the doorway, hoping to be beckoned further.

Gold Eyes lifted a hand up and closed his open jaw.

I was frozen, unsure of what he wanted. Was he waiting to see if I'd turn back to see the open briefcase? What had he said before?

Condition.

"Take me away," I said and hoped he didn't hear the quiver in my voice. If I looked back into my apartment I would see the briefcase and I didn't want to see. I never wanted to see, and so I didn't.

I closed my eyes and then I felt the feathers and how they were varied. Some were soft and some rough. They didn't need to be all one way.

I didn't feel the breeze, though I knew he had lifted off the floor and up through the skylight, as the air outside felt different. It was fresh yet tainted by the same ashy smell. Then a loud siren bellowed through the air.

Suddenly, something felt strange on my foot, I reached down and pulled a large, bright orange sticker off of it. Most of the words were faded, but I managed to make out two words just before the wind took away the sticker.

Two words which I hadn't remembered reading or hearing before.

But of course, I had known them. It's why the apartment building was so quiet.

I was the only one left.

Eviction Notice.

I didn't have to look down to see the destruction of my former home. The sound of the explosion was enough to fill my eyes in, so I looked up at Gold Eyes and he smiled.

The world with its vibrant blue sky gave way to darkness. I could feel something approaching, still I didn't look away from Gold Eyes. I couldn't. He was everything and I was nothing.

His smile vanished as the feeling grew into splashes of gold rippling into the dark.

His blood. My darkness.

I felt his grip loosen and I closed my eyes, hoping and praying to land in my bed. *Please, please please;* I begged as loud as I could without opening my mouth.

The ground appeared beneath my feet and I fought the urge to snap my eyes open. It was a lie. It had to be. I felt reeds of tall grass at my hands. They danced along my skin, rustling in the wind. Beyond the breeze, I felt a presence nearby. Someone large, from the sound of their heavy footfalls.

After taking a large breath, I opened my eyes. "Holy shit," I spun around taking in the vastness of the golden field I was in. The only thing nearby was a tall black spire that shot upwards in a twisted branch-like fashion. It unsettled me, though it was the lesser of the two evils. The fields stretched out farther than my mind could process. There was an-other thud.

Ten feet from me was a giant man, at least he appeared to be a man, and as hard as I tried to search for answers in his face, there were none. Absolutely expressionless. He had eyes that appeared some how harder than the rough skin that refused to respond to the bright sunlight.

I raised a hand and said, "Where are we?"

He mouthed the words, "The fields." And then he smiled. It slithered across his mouth like a snake, then he lowered his shoulders in a fluid motion before charging after me.

My feet took off without a second thought and I ran as fast as I could toward the only landmark in sight. The spire. I couldn't look back, but I swore I heard the giant laughing.

My mind raced along with my feet: what the fuck, what the fuck, what the fuck! The thought was endless like the fields, like the spire.

I ran as hard and as fast as I could to the sound of the heavy footfalls behind me, too close, too loud. The giant cackled. I was certain. Did Gold Eyes bring me here on purpose?

At some point, I reached the spire with its twisted metal fence

As I got closer to the spire, I could better make out the fence around it that looked more like razor-wire than a proper structure. I burst through the gates and the giant stopped in his tracks. My body hit the ground with a thud and after a moment, I looked back at my pursuer. His eyes were a fiery red and his fists were clenched tight enough to draw blood, but it wasn't red running down his arms. It was darker than anything I'd ever seen. Not liquid like blood, it was more like thick steam. Not wishing to stick around, I rose to my feet and heard a loud creaky grinding sound. I turned toward it just in time to see the monstrous gates of the spire opening to reveal a dimly lit foyer. I heard the heavy footfalls of the giant recede into the distance.

"That's not a good sign."

I cringed and closed my eyes as a high-pitched resonance emitted from inside the spire. I collapsed onto my knees and one word penetrated my mind like a tolling bell. It was so loud. Again and again, it repeated.

DREDGE.

The Cottage

Chapter 1

The cloudy orb cleared as its new user committed life to it. She could see it from where she was because change was her specialty—and magic was change. This was the latest new user activated in the realm known as Earth.

She knew this would happen.

The new user in question was aging as they peered into the glass orb. This exchange was one of life. They passed their life into the inanimate object and requested information.

She watched from her place from within the spire. She called it Pursuit because none of what she had done and will do was without purpose, and soon she'd find others who shared in her desire.

The Wardens were all but destroyed. The authority and respect they once commanded was now hers. Soon the spire would grow until it became a spear. Soon, all would know her name. Its mere utterance would cause fear in all who heard it.

Dredge was her name and she wasn't done changing things.

Chapter 2

Fiona Phillips tapped at the sides of her keyboard, begging for something to come along and pluck her away from this painful assignment about nothing and that certainly would never move anyone or anything. It was the middle of the semester and it was only getting worse. Assignment after assignment was duller than dull. She thought there might be something to the idea that a person with an above average IQ was not meant for police work, but this was writing—it should be something more.

The journalism she wanted to contribute to was the kind that changed something. She pledged herself to the idea that her unique perspective could be beneficial to the public at large, which first manifested itself as following in her father's footsteps, but that proved to be an insult to herself. At least that was the idea she stuck to after quitting the police academy on her second day. Her father's legacy was his own. She was unique in her own right and though people like to say that she looks like her mother, with her father's eyes, all in all she counts herself lucky. Except when it came to this journalism assignment. What fluttered out of her mind and onto the laptop screen is a page and a half about how lucky she is.

Lucky that her parents were her parents because it resulted in her skin being light enough that she was able to pass in the white world. It was out of necessity, not because she was ashamed of herself or her parents. Though they could be a lot, that's just what parents were for.

She deleted the words after barely reading a third of them. Knowing these thoughts well enough, Fiona didn't want to be another person explaining to white folks that racism was real. A notification pinged just as she put her hand to the top of the screen to shut the laptop and move on to another screen for the rest of the night. Then her phone vibrated three times. She glanced at the clock and saw that it was nearly midnight, which meant that of course it was *The Signal*.

Back in high school when they got their first cell phones, Fiona and her best friend Anita came up with the secret signal to notify one another of a dire situation. First the email then the three texts, one right after the other. It'd been used when Anita's parents were in a car crash and she thought she had lost her mother. And of course, the night before Fiona's second day of police academy when she talked through everything with Anita and came to the decision that she'd quit and estrange herself from her parents.

As Fiona picked up her phone, she realized that they had effectively swapped turns using the signal which meant that it was Anita's turn. No, that wasn't right. It didn't matter. She was exhausted from too many hours studying, which felt like a sheer cliff built of annoyance.

She unlocked her phone and saw the three texts. Each a solitary word.

You. Need. 2Call.

It was a cheat, but that was Anita, through and through. She tapped on Anita's name which Fiona had in her phone as "My Constant Anita". They were both repulsed by the idea of BFFs. Constant was a word that described it much better. They were each other's rocks.

The phone barely had time to register the full sound of a ring before Anita picked up.

"Hey, any luck with the bullshit?"

Fiona grumbled.

"I tried to wait as long as I could. I know you'd love a distraction, but I also know—"

"Anita. You know I hate—"

"Yeah, yeah, out with it."

Simultaneously, they said, "Miss you constantly, Constant."

"Do you remember Ethan Brahm?" Anita asked. Even though they both knew she didn't need to.

"What is it?"

Anita was silent for a moment, "Well—"

"Did something—" Fiona can't bring herself to finish the question because she doesn't have to ask it. She knew damn well that something had happened because Ethan was a pillar of their group in high school. Anita knew that there was nothing that could erase him from Fiona's memory, so the fact that she asked was proof that she didn't know how to say what had happened.

"I'm not sure. I will send you the obituary."

The word dropped onto her like a ton of bricks. She felt her knees sag, though she remained in her chair. Which she was glad for because surely, she would have collapsed if she had been standing.

"I'm sorry, Na. I wish—"

Fiona exhaled and said, "It's okay. It's not your fault I'm stunned."

"When was the last time you spoke?"

"At least a year and a half. It was hard to—Should I have tried harder?"

"Na, don't do that. It wasn't your responsibility to make sure he grieved properly. Do you know some-body called Casey Gray?"

Fiona sniffled, "Casey Gray? No, I don't think so. Why?"

"That's who was listed on the obituary. I guess they are putting on the funeral. Or at least did."

"When is it?"

"It was today, I just found out about it myself. I'm sorry."

"Send me the link."

"It's in the email, Na."

"When was the last time you saw him?"

"About five months ago, I think. He looked good. I didn't tell you. I'm—"

"Stop apologizing, An. It's not your fault. I know you didn't mention it because you didn't want to stir anything up. And if he was looking good and you told me that I would have... acted."

"I know you loved him, but you were terrible together. Try to remember that."

"Love is love, An. It's a stupid excuse, but it's true. We're animals."

"Only sometimes," Anita hissed.

They both burst out laughing.

"Remember his hair junior year?"

"The emo-phase!"

The laughter continued and they spent hours reminiscing about the old days. It was the most fun Fiona has had in a long time, and she knew before she said it that her words would destroy it, but she had to.

"I'm driving down in the morning."

"Fiona, I don't think you need to. You should stay and study."

"An, listen to me, I need this. I need to say good-bye."

"You've done that already, dear."

"But that wasn't forever."

Anita groaned. "You want to be a journalist; you need to stay put and finish your degree. Ethan isn't going anywhere."

"I owe him," Fiona said barely hanging onto her composure.

"You don't. You got out of this town for a reason, you can't come back and risk being drawn back in."

She didn't have to mention the Tavern. It loomed over everything in Rendbury. Nobody really talked about it, but it was there just out of sight, lurking like a thick fog off of the coast. She hadn't thought about it in some time and now that it was on her mind she understood why she felt different after being away from Rendbury for so long. It'd been less than two years and she had become used to not feeling like the world was pushing her down.

"You're wasting your breath and you damn well know it." Fiona said.

"You're just like your father."

"I can't change that."

"You could try."

Fiona didn't reply.

"Na, come on. You're not pissed at me."

"Stop telling me who I am and what I am. Do you really think that there is any response besides coming home that I'd do with this news? You know me, and I know you. Why are we fighting then?"

"I miss you, Na. I just don't want you getting hurt again."

"I won't. I can come home without seeing them."

Anita burst out laughing.

"What? I'm serious."

"That's why it's funny!"

"You should get some rest. I'll see you in a few hours."

"No, you should sleep first."

"Again, you know me better than that."

"Fine," Anita said with a sigh.

Fiona shifted in her desk chair and rolled her neck. "I'll be fine. It's only a couple hours' drive, no big deal."

"You'll be safe."

"Yes, of course."

"And you'll call me as soon as you get in."

"Text, call, and three knocks."

"You better."

"Love you, Anita. Glad you called even if it was..."

"Love you too, Na. And don't worry, I'm glad we could reminisce. It feels good."

They both disconnect from the call simultaneously. Fiona immediately felt guilty for grinning. It's stupid because he always told her that no matter what he wanted to know she was smiling. The thought brought the tears. The asshole wasn't supposed to be dead. How could he be dead? She plopped her head against the desk and let the tears flow, unable to cease or even think of ceasing them.

Chapter 3

Rendbury was about two hours away from the University of Connecticut, but she may as well have been on a different planet and while she felt it, she didn't realize that was the grip of the Tavern.

The drive went a lot smoother than she could have hoped for. Then again it was the middle of the night, hardly anybody was on the interstate which was great because she hated driving on it and as she passed the prison, she thought and wished that he had found himself there instead. At least she could visit then. Though, would she? Not likely because it would change her view of him drastically and she doubted that she could face him like that.

Can't face the dead.

She killed the engine of her ancient Toyota and closed the door gently before approaching Anita's parent's home. She still lived at home because it was cheaper and her parents weren't overbearing, or at least Anita didn't mind as much as Fiona did. She fired off the text and then hit Anita's name on the display to call her as she made the trek up the two concrete steps that separated the well maintained lawn, before the six strides to the door.

It was strange being back, which she knew it would be and she did her damnedest to not dwell on it much on the ride over. But now it was impossible to ignore. She'd been here countless times—The Belliard's never moved. They bought the house soon after getting married and they've been here ever since. Closing in on thirty years.

The door swung open and Anita burst out, destroying the immediacy of the weirdness gripping Fiona. Their friendship had muscle memory and Fiona was glad that despite the distance they remained this tight. The quiet hug lasted a few moments and Anita pulled away. Fiona furrowed her brow.

"Hey, you know I have to get ready for work soon."

"Right. Sorry." Fiona rolled her shoulders to mask how much this hurt.

"Fiona. You thought I was gonna—"

"No, no—I didn't expect you to drop everything for me."

"It's only eight hours. We can go to the cemetery after I get off. You need to sleep so it's perfect, *actually*."

Fiona nodded, but inside she was screaming because there was no way, no possible way she was going to sleep or rest at all until she faced him. She kept thinking that way and it was wrong, but there was no other way to phrase it. She was going to face him even though she knew she couldn't face the dead.

As Anita got ready for her bullshit secretary job, Fiona found herself looking at pictures in the living room, before long Anita's mother emerged in the doorway.

"Fiona, my dear. Come here, we've missed you." Mrs. Belliard squeezed Fiona in one of the hugs that she wished her own mother was capable of.

"Miss you too, Mrs. Belliard."

"I'm sorry about Ethan," she said touching Fiona's cheeks. "Are you two going to see him today?"

"Yeah, I think when An gets off."

"You're going to wait until then?" Mrs. Belliard was flabbergasted.

Fiona nodded.

"Honey, no. Absolutely not. I will drive you as soon as Anita leaves." Then she winked.

They both wished Anita a lovely day and stood on the front steps, waving as she left for work in the family station wagon. Which Fiona always found strange seeing as they would only need a sedan for the three of them.

"I thought you were going to drive me?"

"Indeed I am, but not in the station wagon."

"You have my attention."

Mrs. Belliard pressed a button on a key ring she produced from her cardigan pocket and the garage door rolled back, revealing a shining blue Thunderbird from the late '70s.

Fiona's mouth dropped open. "Is that? No way!"

Mrs. Belliard's smile beamed.

"Why did you—" She couldn't get through the question. A flood of memories, most prominently the sound of Ethan's laughter overwhelmed her entire person until she bent over, gripping her knees. He wasn't bad. She made a horrible mistake. She should be dead instead of him. He was—

A hand on Fiona's shoulder calmed her and she rose to her feet to look at Mrs. Belliard. She was beautiful and Fiona didn't think the woman had aged much since Fiona was in high school. It didn't make sense, but maybe it was the result of a healthy marriage.

"Fiona, my dear, we loved you two. Truly."

Fiona turned to her best friend's mother and fell onto her, hugging her for all she was worth. "Thank you for this moment. These tears—I can't explain. It all means the world to me."

They stayed like that for a while and then Mrs. Belliard said, "Do you want to drive it?"

Fiona bit her lip and nodded. Ethan never let her drive, but she nodded anyway and rushed to the driver's side of the car. The tears came back full force when she turned the engine over. Another flood of images caught her off guard, she was happy she was sitting because it would have knocked her over otherwise.

She remembered his stupid grin every time he turned the car over. It was like he was king of the world. And he was right. Kings can have flaws. So can best friends. She shook her head, pushing that thought away.

Again, she shook her head and got out of the car. It was too much. Mrs. Belliard seemed to understand and took over.

They didn't say much on the drive. Fiona was taking in the sights of her hometown. Somehow it was the same, just as she left it.

Does anything age here?

The cemetery was a town over in Kestrel, though not far. When the car stopped at the entrance, Fiona looked at Mrs. Belliard and managed, "Casey Gray. Do you know anyone called Casey Gray?"

Mrs. Belliard nodded. "Ethan's sponsor. I've asked him to meet us here. Or rather, to meet you here."

They looked ahead to another blue sedan and saw a man get out and wave to them. Mrs. Belliard spread her hand in a slight wave from the grip of the steering wheel.

"Dear, you'll be okay with him. He was so excited to know you came by."

Fiona looked at her and then back to the man, Ethan's sponsor. Of course, she wanted to pick his brain and learn how it was a sponsor arranged the sponsee's funeral. Where was Ethan's family? Then she remembered his dad. And it all came crashing back.

A pang of guilt rose, she had blocked him out after his dad's funeral when Ethan became too much. She needed more from him than he was capable of and that was clear. She had things she needed to do. Things that needed her attention more than fixing her high school boyfriend. Anita had been there for her and said all these things to her. But in Fiona's mind she always expected and believed that she'd get back to Ethan; after growing up some their love could be even stronger. It was a wonderful thought that got her through the hard quiet nights where every thought exploded through her mind like fireworks.

She hated fireworks, but she loved watching Ethan enjoy fireworks. He was a little kid. And to think he had a sponsor. That was weird. Like how Anita had a full-time job—no, a career. They were growing up and Ethan—

If the Tavern was really meant to protect the people of Rendbury, it was doing a hell of a job.

"Fiona, dear, I promise Casey is good people. It'll help to talk to him. You'll be able to fill in some gaps. Ethan had grown up. He was..." She wasn't able to finish, but Fiona understood intimately what she was thinking.

"He was going to be a great man." It wasn't hard for her to say. It was the truth. Her truth. There was no other way she was coming back to Rendbury... and yet things did change.

Mrs. Belliard cried and Fiona gripped her hand. Fiona wished there was an answer, but she knew there wasn't. There was just... facing the dead.

Fiona finally said, "You'll come back for me?"

"Of course, I have a coffee date with my husband." Mrs. Belliard perked up at the idea and her smile was like a wave. It crashed upon Fiona and soaked her broken heart.

It felt more like alcohol than balm.

Chapter 4

Fiona stood and wished Mrs. Belliard a pleasant time and gently closed the door behind her. Then she lifted a hand toward Casey Gray, who was a man of average height, with some extra weight around his waist and mid-section. He looked tired even from this distance, while his hair was in desperate need of a trim, and perhaps a comb. All in all, he seemed harmless and very average. There was a very light mist falling, but it didn't seem like the weather knew if it wanted to rain or not. As she got closer, he clicked his key fob and his car chirped. The first thing she saw beyond his averageness was his eyes, and that's when she knew what little guard she was carrying had dropped.

"He's this way," Casey said before clearing his throat. "The rain should hold off."

They walked slowly and silently all the way to Ethan's grave which wasn't far from where Casey had parked, maybe twenty-five paces. She didn't mean to count, but it could've been narrated by some aging sports announcer for added drama.

Every step was harder than the last and yet she managed. Of course she did.

The gravestone was a modest one and Fiona had a hard time looking at anything but the hard edges of it. Unable to speak or move past those hard edges, she watched Casey drop to a knee and place his hand on the top of the stone. "Hey kid, I brought someone this time." He looked up at her. "Helps me if I speak to him. I've been here every day since, and I don't see that changing anytime soon."

"Did he... talk about me?"

Casey nodded once. "I don't know your whole story, but I know that he was deliberately putting off seeing you until he was strong enough. Those were the words he used. When I asked him what he meant, he told me that you were disappointed in him and he needed to be drastically different the next time he saw you because that was the only way you'd know how much you meant to him. He didn't want to leave any question in your mind."

She gulped. "How do you know all of that?"

"He told me. When he was having a hard time, especially in the first six months, I would remind him of you. That's why he told me because he needed a reason and you were that reason, Fiona. I'm sorry..." He said looking down at the grave.

"I'm glad you're here, Casey."

"Everyone calls me Gray."

"I like that. Gray." She forced a smile and looked at Ethan's name on the grave marker. There it stood with its large block letters, cold and still, like him — Ethan Brahm. It crushed her to see his name there, etched in the stone like how he was etched into her soul.

"It's my fault."

Fiona whipped her head toward Gray.

He was shaking his head. "Sorry, I'm—uh... the thing is, I know it's not my fault, but I'm gonna keep blaming myself. At least I'm aware of it. That's what my wife says. She's glad for that. He died the night he received his one-year chip. I was really proud, but my wife went into labor and we were having problems, but we were heading in the right direction. I should have backed away from sponsoring him, but I didn't. He was my friend and I enjoyed his company. I didn't want to lose him to someone else. I was selfish."

Gray sat back on the grass and sighed. "Fiona, he was struggling and I didn't know because I had my own things."

"What do you mean struggling? Did he—"

"No, no, definitely not that. He was killed in the woods."

Fiona's jaw dropped. It couldn't be. No way.

"Have you ever heard of Wick's Tavern?"

Her body swayed and Gray jumped to catch her, but she didn't fall. "Wait. No that's... that's not possible."

"So, you have?" His eyes remained innocent and a little confused. He really didn't know.

"Of course. We all have."

Gray shook his head.

"It's a local legend." Fiona said, doing her best to not have to explain it to a newcomer.

"That's why. I just moved to the area roughly two and half years ago. Care to enlighten me?"

She shook her head, locked eyes with Gray and let out a sigh. "Okay. Fine. They say the Tavern is there to protect the town. Someone a long time ago made some deal with someone. Of course, as a kid I heard all sorts of crazy things. People go for a drink and the proprietor judges and... and that's it. You're never seen again. So it doesn't make sense, he knew those stories. He heard it same as me. I shouldn't even being saying this."

"So, you are thinking what? You think he went out there to have a drink?" The color washed out of Gray's face. He was ashamed to even think it.

"I don't... I don't know. It's a story. It's supposed to be a story!" The stories ran through her mind. She'd heard one about a giant made of shadow, but she knew that was impossible. She looked at Gray and cleared her throat. "How do you know he was near the Tavern?" Her voice cracking through the question.

"It was in the police report."

"Police report? What happened?"

"Ethan was attacked by a wild animal. A cop found him."

"Do you know the cop's name?"

"No, when I went in to claim him, they gave me some of the details and some of those were explicitly clear when I saw him on the slab." Gray stood up and took Fiona's hand. "I'm sorry, Fiona. I don't mean to talk about him like that."

"No, it's okay. You're not talking about him; you're talking about his body."

"You believe in the afterlife?"

Fiona smirked and shrugged. "Yeah, I think so. It's a little silly to talk about, I think. I'm not religious, but yeah, I don't think it's over when your body dies. It can't be."

Gray looked at his phone and said, "My wife. I promised her I wouldn't be long. I should go. Will you be okay?"

"Yeah, I'll call my friend's mom and she'll pick me up."

"If you want to talk, I'm always around." They exchanged numbers and Gray walked to his car, leaving Fiona alone at Ethan's grave.

She stared down at Ethan's name. "Why were you there? You fucking know better." She slapped her hand on the grave after she heard Gray's car pull out of the driveway. It didn't make any sense. There was no way that Ethan would have gone out there. He wouldn't have even driven down the road, let alone sit at the Tavern. Did he have a drink at the Tavern? On the night of his one-year sobriety? It didn't make any sense.

She had to speak to the cop that found him, which was a problem because she hadn't been to the precinct since she'd quit and disappointed everyone. Most of all her father, the former captain of the department.

But that didn't matter, at least not more than Ethan did. She could face anyone, except maybe the Tavern. She couldn't imagine Ethan going out there and she sure as hell couldn't imagine herself going out there. Hopefully the officer would have something that would put her at ease.

Chapter 5

The Kestrel police headquarters, which housed all the police for both towns, was a ten-minute walk down the road and she could call Mrs. Belliard when it was time to be picked up and meet her at the cemetery, no problem. No one would even know where she had gone. As she walked, she played over all the times as a young girl when her mother brought her to visit her father at work, once he was taken off the beat. Not that this town was large enough to require a beat or anything like that. Her mother was protective. Maybe a shade overprotective, but most kids feel that way. There were happy memories of the precinct, but the most recent ones were the opposite. She had quit. Day two of police academy, she threw in the towel and never looked back.

It was not a difficult decision, but hindsight is clearer.

There was no one on her side. She saw it from the jump and her idea was to make a friend day one, a friend that would carry her through and together they would change it from within. She needed a friend because there was no way she could do it on her own. No way in hell. But everyone there was through and through police. They were there for the culture. The white-hot stomping brutality. She hated all that shit. The chest out, tough guy bullshit.

She was getting herself all riled up and had to slow it down before she came up on the precinct and burned the fucking place down. She stopped and closed her eyes and let everything fall away. Visiting the police HQ wasn't about her or her father, but she sure as hell was going to use all of that to her advantage. No way the officers would ignore or write her off.

The precinct was a dark building on a slight hilltop, it overlooked much of the town and seeing it made her skin crawl. Kestrel wasn't Rendbury. While there were a few officers dedicated to Rendbury, it was really one police force for the two towns and for a time it was her father who oversaw it all. Prior to his retirement, he'd hoped to leave it all to her, but she ruined that.

Fiona continued and didn't stop again until told to wait by the officer at the front desk. He recognized her, but something else had caught her eye already. There was an officer coming out of the bathroom, profusely sweating and he jumped when the front desk officer called his name. Kerry Hayes.

It sounded familiar, but everyone in a small town has a familiar name. This young officer was maybe the same age as her, but there was something off about him.

"How can I help you, Miss Phillips?"

She walked across the room and offered him her hand. "Good afternoon, Officer Hayes. I wanted to ask you about Ethan Brahm. I hear you are the one that found him."

"There's not much to tell, to be honest." He coughed in his hand to hide his unsteady voice.

"I'd like to hear it. Have you eaten lunch?"

"I have, ma'am. It's not a long story. I can give you the bird's eye view."

She nodded once.

"How about you come to my desk and we can talk."

"Sure. Thanks."

He held his hand out showing her the way. She obliged, knowing that he wanted to walk behind her. Most likely for multiple reasons; he was attracted to her, it was obvious, but also there was something else about his face. Something going on deeper behind his eyes than just attraction. Something dark.

There was no reason for her to use that word other than instinct. A cop's hunch, her father would have said.

Once they sat, it became clearer. She watched as he spread his legs and began touching himself—lightly at first. Rubbing his crotch and leaning his head back. She cleared her throat, but he didn't notice. He groaned and she said, firmly, "Officer Hayes."

He jolted awake. There was no other word for it. He shook his head and noticed his hand was on his crotch and he quickly removed it.

"Yeah, sorry. You have questions?" He said quickly shifting focus back to her. He reached for his water bottle, took a long swig and then coughed. He couldn't cease the cough; he got up and pointed to the bathroom.

Fiona sighed as she watched the piss poor officer hurry to the bathroom. The idiot forgot he spiked his water with vodka and damn near choked himself to death. She could tell that he lost himself somewhere along the way after checking her out, not that it made much sense. It was gross, but it was far down her list of things to let get to her today. She needed to talk to this idiot cop. Not sure where the surprise came from, she was well acquainted with cops and was pretty close to becoming one if making it through one day of police academy was considered close; she supposed it was because most never even dream of attempting police academy. But her father was her father, and that seemed to be the route to go. Despite her mother's wishes, she was never going to be a proper girl. Not professionally and not with her pixie cut, but that wasn't for her mother to decide or determine. It was up to her and only her to find out who Fiona Phillips was.

After a few moments, the idiot boy returned which was good because it was getting hard to resist the openly logged in computer.

"You all right, Officer Hayes?"

The idiot nodded groggily.

"Are you still up for some questions?"

Again, he nodded.

"Gonna need you to speak though, That okay?"

"Yeah," He managed inside of a groan.

"I don't want to waste your time, Officer. So, I'll just cut right to it. What were you doing when you found him? How did it happen? Take me through it. If you could." Fiona batted her eyelashes, knowing that it would get her exactly what she wanted. She'd worry about how it made her feel later.

Officer Hayes cleared his throat. "It's a little hard to talk about exactly. How about I get you the report instead and you can read it, and then ask me questions about it some other time?"

"You'd make me a copy of the report?" She asked with her big green eyes focused solely on his own, dull grayed.

"Yeah, just give me a minute."

As he walked away, she shook her head. This was way too easy. Are all cops like this?

He returned with a manila folder and said, "Don't read it here."

"Wouldn't dream of it, thank you Officer," She exited the precinct, produced her phone from her pocket. Looking out across the way, she could almost see the cemetery from this vantage point. It was only his body. Maybe it was the stories, maybe it was something else, all she knew was she felt certain that grave was not the end. She called Mrs. Belliard and as the phone rang, she thought it was a good thing the visit to the precinct didn't take all that long.

Chapter 6

Ethan's car roared up the road, Fiona's mind spiraled through all the times she waited for him to pick her up. For a moment, she let herself believe that he was behind the wheel. She closed her eyes and saw him behind the wheel, smile bigger than the street.

The brakes squeaked slightly, as the car came to a stop.

"Fiona, dear?" Mrs. Belliard called through the open window.

After a moment, Fiona opened her eyes and did her best to smile. Then she got in the car, his car. Luckily, she had the folder to grip or else she'd dig her nails into her palms.

Mrs. Belliard didn't ask about the folder or anything really. Her husband was only home for a few hours and then he was back to work. There was some big business deal going down in Chicago, and he managed a rather lengthy layover in NYC so he could spend a couple hours with his wife before he was gone again. It was a rough deal, but she took it well enough.

"I'm glad you got to see your husband for a bit today, Mrs. Belliard."

"Aren't you the sweetest?" She glanced at Fiona and smiled. "Don't you worry about me; I can't imagine what you're going through."

"We weren't together."

"I know, but you should have been. I'm sorry other people didn't agree."

"She was looking out for me."

"Where is she now?"

Fiona looked out the window. "That's your daughter, you know."

"Fiona, I know her well. She's part of me, but that doesn't mean that every part of me is right about everything all the time."

"Come on now. Let's ask Mr. Belliard."

She smiled. "Trained is different. Speaking of, how are your studies going?"

"It's difficult. I spent most of my life looking toward police work. It's hard to wrap my head around the idea that it's not for me."

"All the more reason for you to keep something certain around." She showed a knowing smile.

"Mrs. Belliard, I love you for being this way. I really do. But let's think about this for a moment; if I had stayed with Ethan, where would we be? Two people struggling together doesn't really make a good fit. It sounds okay, but when neither person is able to be available for the other then it's nothing. I love your daughter, she's my best friend. Nothing can change that. She wasn't wrong. And she wasn't right either. It's hardly ever cut and dry like that. She was looking out for me and that's what I choose to focus on. I'd appreciate it if you didn't down her decision, her advice. For all we know, that's what saved me." Fiona felt the words spilling out faster and faster, when she stopped, she wept, her hands shielding her face. Fiona felt the car stop and a hand reach over to her.

"Fiona, honey, look at me."

Fiona looked up at the woman that has been a mother to her without ever needing to be. She had a mother. But she lucked into another. Fiona knew she was lucky.

"I don't disagree with my daughter. I just thought maybe you needed to vent. I'm sorry for assuming such a thing. You're a hell of a lot stronger than I would be in this situation. I thought that's why she went to work today, to hide from facing Ethan."

"No, we're okay. I wanted her to indulge me, but I think it's better that she didn't. She's looking out for me."

"Was the car a mistake?"

"No, gosh no, Mrs. Belliard. I love it. Thank you so much. I just can't—"

"I understand. I have to hide Mr. Belliard's dining room chair when he's away. I can't bear to see the chair empty. I thought tonight was going to be troublesome when Anita got home from work, but it sounds like everything is good between you two. I wish I had a friend that trusted my judgment the way you trust hers. I'm impressed by you, Fiona."

The car started again and a minute later they were pulling in the driveway where Anita was waiting on the front steps. She ran toward the car overflowing with surprise.

"Mom, what are you driving?" A second later she corrected herself, "This is Ethan's."

"Your mom is the greatest," Fiona said, reaching for Anita through the open window.

"Na, we need to talk. Mom, do you mind?"

"Not in the slightest, I was thinking of dinner. Anything you girls want?"

"Doesn't really matter, as long as it's food." Fiona said, smiling.

The two girls watched Mrs. Belliard wave and walk through the front door. Anita opened the car door for Fiona and they walked around the back of the house to where so many adventures took place. Camp-outs in a flimsy tent. The first talks about boys. The usual topics. Even the fabled, "Why don't we just marry each other?"

They sat on the red picnic table facing the woods out back and almost immediately Fiona began picking at the peeling paint.

Anita didn't look at Fiona, she just spoke. "Fiona, you can't go out there. I know where you went today and I need you to promise me."

"What are you talking about?" Fiona grabbed at Anita, but she pulled away.

"Don't. Don't you dare." She said as she slid away.

"What?"

"I don't know why he went out there, but you can't. Okay? You just can't. People go in those woods and they don't come out."

"I met the cop that did."

"And how does he look?" Anita said, making sure her face was turned away from Fiona.

"What does that mean?"

"Fiona."

It was meant to be final, but Fiona couldn't let this go. "You fucking know something. Anita, look at me."

Anita turned and her deadly gaze shocked Fiona, nearly off her seat. "Happy now?" Her eyes were cloudy white and her brow had more wrinkles than an ocean has waves. It was clearly Anita, but she was fifty years older. The crow's feet at her eyes screamed in pain. In a raspy voice that Fiona barely recognized, Anita said, "I looked because I wanted to know."

"What are you talking about?" Fiona reached toward her friend's face, and was deflected by Anita's shriveled hand.

"I met this man that had a book about orbs and how different ones are good for different things. He had one for looking and I looked. I've been trying to undo it, but it's no use. If I concentrate hard enough, I can hide it, but it's exhausting. I'm going to have to leave town and I want you to come with me."

Fiona raised her hands, "Anita, I don't understand. You looked at what?"

"I looked in the orb and saw how he died."

"You know what you're saying makes no sense."

Anita nodded. "He said that I had to surrender myself to the magic to make the orbs work. I had no idea he was serious."

"You have to show me."

"No, I don't! Don't make me cry, it hurts my eyes and I'm afraid. The orb is gone. I smashed it when I saw him... He was my friend too."

"The cop gave me the police report."

"Isn't that illegal?"

Fiona nodded. "He wants to fuck me."

"Oh my god, Na."

"God has no place here."

"We should just go. Please, Fiona. Let's go and forget about this bullshit town."

"What about your family?"

"What about yours?"

"Fair. Do you know why he went out there? Did he forget?"

"Nobody forgets about Wick's."

"Then why?"

"I don't know that he had a choice."

"You think it called him?"

"The Tavern doesn't call, it only judges." Anita said in a flat tone.

"The stories can't all be true." Fiona said, knowing the words were not true. She believed because she had felt it as soon as she returned to Rendbury.

"Fiona, look at me. It's all true. Tell me about the cop."

"He looked horrible like he was rotting from the inside."

"He'll go back. It's got to be guilt or something."

"Guilt? What did you see?"

"Let's look at that report and I'll tell you what it got wrong."

Fiona produced the folder from her purse and gave it to Anita. She watched as her friend squinted and quickly flipped through the pages.

"Here, this is the officer's first-hand account. It says, that he discharged his weapon at a wild animal that was mauling Ethan. I'll skip the details and just give you the—whoa, this is all kinds of wrong. What I saw was more than one thing in the woods. So did the officer because he used a whole clip or magazine or whatever they call it. Then he must have realized what he'd done and reloaded, then fired two shots. He stated in the report that he fired two shots and that was it. He lied. Why would he lie?"

"If he used a whole magazine then that's a full investigation. He'd be suspended and the whole nine. Psych eval too. He's a young cop and something like that early on would probably result in him being booted off the force or at least hung out to dry. The department wouldn't have much to lose there. He isn't a decorated veteran, just some kid."

"So, he lied to protect his job?"

"And to protect his reputation surely. Because if you saw—"

"A pack of weird little critters like small feral children."

"Yeah, I wouldn't go on record saying that as a cop. He'd surely be ostracized. But why not grab one of the bodies as proof? It doesn't make sense if he killed one. He must have killed at least one if he fired off a whole clip."

"They look like kids."

"Christ, you're right."

"So now you know. We can leave," Anita said closing the folder.

"The hell we can. He lied. He's a cop. He needs to pay for that."

"Fiona, please."

"An, I'm serious. I can't just leave knowing what happened. He needs to be investigated properly. He hid evidence!"

Anita sighed. "But you know what's going to happen to him. It really doesn't matter if you get involved."

"What are you talking about?"

"He went into those woods and returned. What do you think is going to happen?"

"Exactly why he needs to be watched."

"Fiona, he doesn't need to be watched." Anita paused and stared straight into Fiona's eyes, "All you have to do is wait outside the Tavern."

"Anita, what is going on? There's something you aren't saying."

She shook her head. "He left the woods. That's never happened before. He will return. Bet on it."

Fiona looked at her friend and saw that she was right. She knew what she was talking about. How was not something that Fiona could ask. It didn't matter. She was going to the Tavern. She swallowed and tried to hide the shudder. It didn't matter because Anita was distracted, as she focused her energy on creating the youthful facade. She was using magic of some sort. They would talk about it when all of this was settled.

For now, there was no time to waste. Fiona told Anita to say goodbye to Mrs. Belliard for her and that she'd be back later to eat whatever leftovers they couldn't finish. The food would not be wasted, she made sure Anita was going to promise it. Then she took Anita's car and headed for the strange country road and the stranger Tavern.

Chapter 7

Fiona gripped the steering wheel of the Belliard's station wagon tighter than she thought possible. She could barely believe she was heading to the Tavern. She told herself to focus on finding a place to stash the car. The winding narrow road offered plenty of places to hide a vehicle. She chose one little dirt spot roughly five hundred feet from the Tavern. She could just barely see the light from the doorway around the corner. So, anyone entering or exiting the place could not see her vehicle unless something shone down on the reflective surfaces. She crossed the street and squatted in the woods ten feet from the street, her view of the Tavern was clear, but anyone coming or going wouldn't be able to see her. She hoped.

Eventually she changed to a sitting position, watching as nothing happened. No one came or went. The light never flickered. It was stagnant like a fucking pond. She glanced at her watch which glowed dully, hardly enough to give away her position. If she checked her phone, it'd be as effective as

a flare gun. The watch read nearly 3am. She was exhausted and about ready to give up when she heard a
fast-approaching car. It was the only one she'd heard
all night. It slid around the bends and barely came to
a stop at the Tavern's entrance. She thought for sure
the little Civic was going to collide with the building.

She watched a young man stumble out of it. Officer Kerry Hayes.

He was in the Tavern for all of ten minutes
and then quickly stumbled out again, nearly falling
down the tall staircase to the entrance. Even from
this distance, she could hear the prick muttering to
himself. He ignored the car, to her surprise, and
made his way down the road a ways until he ducked
into the woods. It looked as if he was swallowed by
the trees. She rose from her position and made her
way to the Tavern. As she climbed the stairs, the light
went out, and she looked up to the doorway in time
to see the proprietor shake his head and latch the
door. Then he vanished into the darkness.

Trees began moving, and then it sounded as if a
few were torn from the ground and tossed aside.
Fiona inhaled and hustled for the noise. Bound-

ing down the stairs, she leapt down the last few and sprinted toward the woods where Officer Hayes headed.

She slowed as she broke through the tree-line, grabbing the small flashlight from her belt holster. She wasn't a cop, but she was the daughter of one. Fiona clicked it on and slowly scanned upward from her feet, toward the sound of heavy footsteps. She clasped a few fingers over the light to mask the beam. Slowly she trudged through the woods, careful not to break a twig or ruffle any leaves. Her foot placement was perfect. She hated to admit it, but it was because of the grueling ballet training her mother insisted she endure as a child. Proper girls do ballet. Proper girls have long hair.

Fiona was more than happy to be anything but a proper girl. Her mother had no right to her happiness.

As she made her way, she tried to banish the thoughts, the vitriol that she inherited from her father. If she shoved it deep enough it'd never be found. Her grip on the light tightened and began straining her wrist. Her focus was elsewhere and after a few white knuckled moments, her wrist pinged her with a burst of pain causing her to let go. Switching the light off and passing it to her off hand, she shook her right wrist until the pain broke. With a sigh she continued forward, placing the small light back into her right hand, pushing aside the thoughts of carrying a pistol.

Then a twig snapped beneath her feet.

She gasped and heard a thud that made her hair stand up on end. Heavy footsteps echoed through the forest, and she knew whatever it could be was not Hayes. It was something larger. Much larger. They train postal employees to not run from dogs and that's all this was. A big forest dog. She would not run.

A lumbering shadow emerged from the trees and made its way through a small stone wall, erupting the interlocking rocks into a load of rubble. Fiona stumbled backwards as the shadow's left hand shot up. She saw the moonlight glimmer across the shining particles within what appeared to be a large stone arm. The stone perfectly taking the shape of a hand and forearm. Even the elbow and all the way up to the shoulder was stone. It had to be encased in stone. There was no way it was chiseled and made from a boulder.

Bewildered didn't really capture it, Fiona felt like she was both frozen in place and floating far above her body. She was maybe ten feet from a man that was larger than anyone she'd ever seen. If she reached upward, she wouldn't be able to reach his larger than a basketball sized head, which sat right on top of his torso—his neck virtually nonexistent. Under the light from the stream of her flashlight, she saw the roughness to his flesh like that of a rhinoceros, just lighter in color. Fiona saw his rough skin react to the light, his body recoiled slightly, and there was darkness that billowed like steam off of his skin.

She lowered her flashlight, knowing it would only irritate the giant, so she promptly holstered it. The click of her holster sprang through the air, echoing through the woods. The stone armed giant stopped, lowered his own weapon and turned away from Fiona. Then he tilted his head, indicating for her to follow. She looked back the way she came and saw nothing but forest. There was no one coming to her aid. Pain shot through her at the idea of dying alone in the woods.

This was what Ethan felt. Her heart felt like it shattered and the shards tore through her insides. He was swarmed by small creatures and only her and Anita would ever know the truth. Maybe it was better to die by the hands of a giant than live with that secret.

A groan came from nearby and she saw a groggy Officer Hayes stand and continue to groan and growl.

Fiona started towards the giant with the stone arm in time to see him toss Hayes over his shoulder. His service weapon fell to the ground, which she managed to scoop up as she walked by it, all while keeping her distance from the giant. Her hand coiled around the gun and she wished it didn't feel good, but it did. Something about the gun felt strange, it was beating, like something was coursing through it. Fiona turned her hand and the gun toward the moonlight, and shadow billowed off of it like smoke. She nearly dropped it, until she heard the giant's footfalls thudding away from her.

She was Hayes's only backup. She wasn't a cop, but she couldn't erase the years of expectation and intention. It was part of her. Tucking the gun into her waistband at her backside, she took off after the giant and Kerry.

They walked for nearly forty minutes before—despite the weakening moonlight—a destination came into view. It was a small cottage, a sagging roof and plenty of missing siding. It was probably infested with critters and mold. Where Fiona came from, it would be considered a shed. But that was her past, not her present. It seemed like a world away.

The cottage sat atop a small crest of a hill, as if the rest of the forest looked up to it or at least respected it. No green was present on the crest. She didn't think it was dead. This was something else. A significant jolt of fear sprang through her.

The giant stopped and turned back to check if Fiona was still following.

It almost seemed like he cared. How strange. It was clear to her and yet he did not speak. He only made motions that beckoned her onward. She didn't feel safe, but she was sure he would not harm her.

Quietly, they walked up the beaten path to the cottage. There was a fire pit and benches made of split trees. The giant lowered Hayes onto one and faced the door of the cottage, he took a step then sprang around, holding a hand up toward her.

He didn't want her to follow.

She sat on the other bench without looking away from him. He nodded and proceeded carefully inside. There was a flurry of clatters behind the closed door. She didn't flinch. She glanced at Kerry and saw that his chest was rising, albeit faintly. He was in trouble, but she couldn't risk trying to offer aid that would upset their host. All she could do was wait it out.

The door burst open and an old black board on wheels made its way onto the tiny porch. The giant pushing it from behind, he ducked out the door and carefully aligned the board so Fiona could see its entirety. He held a piece of chalk up and smiled. It was a pained expression.

Fiona nearly fell backwards. She coughed and collected herself. The giant slid between the wobbly railing and the chalk board. She heard the rubbing of chalk on the board. The sound slowed until it stopped and he backed away from it. Holding his hands out to the board. The smile had become a grin that she didn't think she'd ever see on a grown man. She realized then that's what he was. He wasn't a giant; he was a man. A big man with a stone arm.

The chalk board read simply, "I am Warden."

The last word had been written with care. She thought this must be his title, not his name. She gazed across the yard into his eyes and saw this man as he was. A man hurting. She wanted to get up and go to him, but knew that he wouldn't take to that.

She nodded at the board finally. Unsure if she should speak since he didn't. She had no way to be sure, but something told her that he couldn't speak. The giant wrote because he had to.

He quickly grabbed the board and wiped it down with his hand made of flesh. The sound of chalk moving fast filled the air. He stepped away revealing what he'd written.

"Speak to me. I trust you."

"Why do you trust me?" She asked.

He went back to the board and after a long moment he backed away.

"You chose not to abandon that poor excuse for a man."

She smiled and saw it returned then asked, "You don't like him?"

The man on the porch shook his head and went to the board.

"He murdered my family. Confessed. He wants to die."

"He said that or you...?" She didn't finish, but saw that the man understood better than she could have put it.

The scritch scratching of the board grew more frantic, but there wasn't worry in it. Not anymore. He was enjoying it.

"He said so. I don't want to be like him. Not anymore."

She swallowed. "Anymore? Have you killed?"

This time he only wrote one word. "Warden."

"I don't understand."

He went to the board once again except there was hesitation, perhaps regret or shame, Fiona couldn't be sure. He probably could convey it fully, but chose not to. This frightened her. He scribbled on the board and backed away in a hurry.

"Easier to show you?" The question mark was especially jagged, more like a scythe than a hook.

She looked at him and she knew how he wanted her to answer, but curiosity could not be clipped off at this point. She nodded slowly. He turned away and slammed the door open, shoving the board back to where it came from and in a quick motion, shut the door and descended down off the porch.

He locked eyes with her, as if checking to make sure she was certain. Then he nodded and made his way back up the stairs.

Stopping before the door, he extended his stone pointer finger, put it to his lips, and winked at her. Fiona smiled and looked back at Officer Hayes; he was still asleep, but she thought she saw him rustle awake. She heard the door and snapped her focus toward it.

Chapter 8

Fiona scanned the room, but her attention was quickly stolen by the sudden stop of her guide. He stopped, looked at her then down to the floor. After a deep breath, she followed his eyes.

The floor was clear, like a window looking into another world. Fiona backpedaled fast, the walls of the cottage were the only thing that kept her upright.

She looked back to the giant, he was finishing a sentence on the blackboard, "I can show you the past."

Fiona followed the chalk in his hand from the blackboard as he pointed to the floor. Through the floor window, she saw a great field that went on for decades. That was the word that came to her. It was about time, not distance. It was overwhelming to look at. How could it go on forever?

Suddenly, the endless gold field was smeared with red. Thick dark red blood. She could nearly smell it. A giant rolled through the field. Fiona couldn't tell if it was her guide or not. Something rocketed through the air that made her think of lightning, and it collided with the giant's arm. She saw the stone encase the flesh and knew who this was. He was speechless and just stared off in the direction he came from. Hurt and horror stained his face. There was a lot, and he wore it all for her to see. The disappointment of an enormous disagreement.

Another giant came from seemingly nowhere, lifting her guide up from the blood-soaked field. The blood was erased and the second giant's voice boomed.

"Don't worry, you'll get used to the weight of your mistakes," He tapped the stone arm. "Warden, time to settle into your new role."

Fiona looked to her guide. "What sort of disagreement gets you... all of this?"

The Warden shook his head.

"What does a Warden do?"

Her guide pointed his hand down to the floor.

The golden field was gone, in its place was a vast hole. Vast was wrong because it implied an end. This hole, like the field, was not measured in size, but in time. The hole's time was shorter. It was turned inside out. She heard scratching on the chalk board and turned to see the Warden holding his hand to a word she didn't recognize.

Sheol.

He pointed to the hole then back to the word. The hole was called Sheol. She watched the hole spiral upward into a tall spire. As it did, she saw small shadows bleed from it, at first only a few then as it grew there were more and more. The shadows reached out from the spire, but were quickly drawn back in by some invisible force. The Warden beside her scratched at the chalk board then tapped at it.

It read: Pursuit.

She said, "The spire."

The Warden nodded then wrote, "Shades tried to escape during the change, but they were unable to. Wardens persuade souls, offering guidance through the fields. Not all realms want wandering souls. So they worked for us, as shades."

"Realms? You mean Heaven and Hell?"

The Warden laughed. He wrote, "Heaven and Hell are stories. Humans love stories."

"So, shades are dark souls?"

The Warden smiled. "Low like the stricat. Workers at best."

She suspected this was wrong, he had just called them family a moment ago. Perhaps, somehow, someone could listen in while they were inside here. "Why are you telling me all of this?" After a moment, she amended, "I'm not taking over for you."

His laughter boomed as he turned to the chalk board.

"Wardens are a bloodline."

"So, I can't take over. I don't have it in my blood?"

He nodded and wrote, "I want you to understand. The other must pay for slaughtering the stricat."

"Kerry?"

The Warden wrote, "He was trying to save the other man."

"He killed him and covered it up and that's why he's been acting strange."

"That's not all," The Warden wrote and pointed towards the door.

She peered out the window and saw Kerry convulsing. She shot a glance back to the Warden. "How does a soul become dark?"

"You already know. That's why you followed."

Fiona opened her mouth to speak, but the Warden held up his hand and erased the board with the other. He was right. She did understand that Kerry was changing. Not that she knew him before, it was just a feeling. An insight into the condition of his humanity, or lack thereof. She wanted clear proof of wrongdoing, that's why she followed, and yet here in this cottage she knew that the Warden was right. There was more to it. More than just Ethan. The classic metaphor came to her mind and for once it may be apt. He was a bad cop that would spoil the whole bunch if left alone.

The board read, "You were curious. That's why we are talking, also why I didn't allow him inside."

She opened her mouth and he put a hand up and quickly wrote, "He is susceptible." Then he erased it and wrote, "Be patient as I write, please."

She agreed and watched as he erased and started from the very top of the board. She was eager, but managed to not read over his shoulder. There was pounding on the door and she turned her head as the Warden tapped on the board to get her attention to where it belonged. He didn't want her looking out there. There wasn't any reason to ask, she knew the answer. By not asking, she allowed herself to believe that she still thought there was hope for Kerry.

Finally, the giant stepped away from the board and put his hands behind his back. She started reading.

"This cottage, along with this arm, is my severance package. I am no longer an active Warden. After a time, I found it to be peaceful. Until the other night when the man outside murdered the stricat, I had come to think of as my family. I expected more than the couple of you, but then I saw him, alone, in my forest. Truthfully, a human weapon is not supposed to be able to kill beings from another realm, but perhaps that's a mystery we won't solve here."

She stopped reading before reaching the end, pulled the gun out from her waistband. The thing billowed with black smoke, or maybe it was more like the spire that she saw earlier. Darkness bleeding off of it.

Before she could say it was Kerry's, the Warden stumbled backwards, his mouth hanging open.

"What is it?"

He quickly erased the first bit of the board and wrote, "It can't be." Then he snatched the gun from her.

"Hey, wait, I can use that kill him. That's what you want isn't it?"

He shook his head then looked around for a place to put the gun. Shaking his head again, he wrote, "There isn't time. She can't have this."

Then he tapped the bottom of the board. Fiona read the words written there.

"It's not as many humans believe. Heaven and Hell are stories. There is a great gold field that either you pass through or you don't. Human stories of possession are not far off. That's the closest to a definition of a dark soul that can be said. When you walk out of that door, your susceptible friend will no longer be the man you remember. Let me be clear, Kerry is gone. He cannot be saved. His soul must leave this realm."

She looked at the Warden. "You're going to kill him?"

He shook his head. Then erased the board.

"She corrupted the Wardens. This is worse than a shade."

"Then what? Tell me what the hell the plan is!"

He took a moment to wipe the board clean and wrote, "Telling you is my plan. This is all I can say."

"What if I go out there and then he kills me?"

He wrote. "What would you have me do?"

"This is bullshit. You're going to do nothing? You let him get turned!"

The Warden stepped toward her, and viciously pointed his stone hand at her. He looked straight in her eyes and mouthed the word no.

"Then what would you call it?"

He went to the board and wrote, "It was already done when he left here the other night. And this is far worse than I thought."

"What does the gun mean? What happened to it?"

The Warden rubbed his stone arm, "Some mistakes cannot be undone or forgiven. Humanity loves forgiveness, but unfortunately that is not the way the rest of us operate. Kerry's dark soul is the result of his deceptions and corruption. It runs deep."

"You're hiding something. You want me to send him to the spire?"

"You are not capable of that. He must go through the field."

"But his soul is dark."

"Sometimes that is an advantage."

"Advantage? What is in the field?"

"I can't tell you."

She scoffed and walked to the door. "Don't I need garlic or something? What do I use to kill him?"

The Warden laughed.

She threw her hands up in frustration, let out an annoyed exhale, and then she opened the door.

Chapter 9

Fiona cringed as the door creaked open and was surprised when she didn't see Kerry anywhere. The bench was vacant and there was no one on the porch. He should be right here. She looked back inside the cottage; the Warden was not moving. She was on her own.

"Officer Hayes? You out here?" After a tick, "Kerry? It's Fiona. Show yourself." She descended the porch stairs and hopped backwards immediately as a growl sounded to her left.

"Would you prefer another name?" She took a step forward. "You've changed so it makes sense. Want me to help you pick a new one?" She dragged her foot up and carefully let it down. Moving all of five inches forward. "Do you still have Kerry's memories? Do you think he knew that I had started... falling for him?" She was surprised when a figure ascended into view. Guys are guys regardless of soul status, apparently.

The figure straightened and twisted itself around and when it stepped forward, the dying moonlight fell upon it and she was struck by how normal Kerry looked. His behavior was all wrong, but it was the same face, the same eyes. Except the shuffle, he dragged his feet along the ground like an incredibly drunk person using a moving sidewalk for the first time. He held his head backwards probably for balance.

Fiona said, "Kerry, it's me Fiona."

"Fiona," He sounded it out, dragging the syllables out longer than her strides had been a moment earlier. He continued, "Put. You. Way." The words were strenuous and terrified Fiona. She wasn't sure he was opening his mouth all the way.

She didn't budge.

Kerry lumbered forward, "AWAY!"

She jumped backward and hoped that she wouldn't trip over the stairs. Luck was on her side.

Kerry shouted again, losing his balance over a small stone. Groaning as he tried to pull himself up and toward Fiona, he shouted again. "Away!"

Fiona dodged to the side, using Kerry's momentum and lack of balance to push him away, sending him stumbling down to the ground.

But he was onto her, she could see it in his eyes. They were Kerry's eyes and Kerry was a cop. She couldn't fool him. He wasn't a zombie. He would be difficult to thwart. Was this the test the Warden had planned?

They walked around in a circle; she took a step and he would follow. One after the other. If only the Warden hadn't taken the gun, then this would be over. Nothing was ever easy. She moved, continuing in the circle and as he followed. A strange sound filled the air, Fiona thought it sounded like a large bird, she chanced a glance at the cottage.

In the doorway was the Warden's free arm, holding a pistol. It looked like an ancient revolver, maybe one of the first. Definitely before the 20th century. Her great grandfather had an antique gun collection and this looked like it could have belonged to it. She remembered something about her great grandfather talking about how he loved the old Colts. Though, his favorite was the Paterson because of their accuracy, and as she drew closer to the open cottage and got a better look at the revolver, it looked like a Paterson from as far as she could tell. The long barrel was the giveaway. She hopped up the stairs and snatched it from the Warden's hand.

A rough hand grabbed the back of her neck and tossed her up and across the small yard. She collided with one of the wooden benches. She gathered herself and looked up at Kerry. Did he get faster? His eyes changed from those she had seen before. These were eyes of something else. She groaned and got to her feet as the former officer shuffled toward her. Fiona gripped the revolver and tried thumbing the hammer back. It didn't budge.

The former officer growled as he came closer. His movements were blurry, like with every passing moment he was getting faster.

Fiona called to him, "Kerry! Stop where you are!"

Kerry didn't stop, he only groaned further while twisting his head. His movements had started to change. There was something different, something inhuman about his twitching movements.

"Officer Hayes, I'm the one with the gun here. I don't want to fire!"

"Lies!" He snarled.

She gripped the gun with both hands and using both thumbs, managed to pull the hammer back. Driving his car was out of the question, and this was even more powerful. What would Ethan think if he saw her holding this cannon? And what about her dad? She felt like a character from the westerns he used to watch on Sunday afternoons. There was justice there, in the old west; a justice not found in the modern day. That's what the Warden was about.

That's what all of this was about. Justice for Ethan.

She heard Anita's voice in her head, "You mean revenge."

"No," she told herself, "death isn't the end."

Fiona glared at her opponent and saw only his flaws. He was a corrupt white cop, a story older than it should be. A story that began in these woods when he covered up what he'd done. Here it would end, not because he was evil, but because he'd done a bad thing and bad things happen over and over again. But she knew that the real fire that burned her insides was Ethan.

Kerry was culpable.

"Kerry Hayes, you were a bad cop before you put on the uniform and the badge. The culture attracts guys like you. It's why I got out when I did. One person can't change it. But one person can deprive people of learning what really happened to a person they loved. That's inhuman. That's you, Kerry. When you did that, you sealed your fate. In this case, I'm glad the Tavern was here to judge you." As soon as she said it, she understood everything. The Tavern did all of this, somehow, someway and she was going to find out why; and maybe through that she'd learn what drove Ethan out here. Whatever that place really was, the Warden would never tell.

Kerry made no sign of understanding what she was on about. He just groaned and continued toward her. She lined the ancient sight up with his abdomen and pulled hard at the trigger. The force shot through her whole body as she watched Kerry's body react to the penetrating shot. It rocketed him back a hair, but he kept coming.

She cocked the hammer back with both hands again and fired. As soon as she did, she readied the gun again. Firing another off in quick succession.

One went wide, while the other one exploded her target's skull. He collapsed toward her and she dodged, dropping her gun and managing to take a few steps backward before falling to her knees. Her sobbing was loud, but not loud enough to block out the sound of the old cottage door. Without turning around, she tried to swallow her sobs and managed through a cracking voice, "Is this what you wanted?"

But there was nothing that followed the sound of the creaking door. No footsteps, or anything at all. Then a crackle of thunder and a large thud on the porch. She whipped her head up and saw what looked like a split open cast. It was his stone arm, split down the middle, lengthwise. No flesh present. His severance package, as he called it, had been removed.

A feeling in her gut told her not to approach the cottage and definitely avoid going inside, yet she also felt drawn. She grabbed the ancient revolver, checked the cylinder—three shots remained—then tucked it in her back waistband. Rising to her feet, she swallowed the last of her crying, but did not wipe her face. She wasn't ashamed of feeling nor was she ashamed of protecting herself. She would answer for what she did.

An odd gust of wind blew the cottage door, banging it against the outside wall as she climbed the porch stairs. She gave the stone cast a wide berth, almost hopping over it. Inside the cottage, there was a message on the chalk board. Fiona saw it without having to enter, but she still crossed the threshold into the small cottage.

"Thank you, Fiona. Your actions proved my status as Warden necessary. Be safe."

The door slammed shut behind her, as the floor changed back into its window like version. She saw the golden field unfold before her eyes. The endless waving grains of the field mesmerized her until a shape came into focus. Kerry.

Fiona watched as he began walking forward, scanning back and forth until he stopped and focused on something that she couldn't see. He cupped his hands around his mouth, presumably yelling for whatever or whoever was there out of Fiona's sight. She desperately wanted to know what he was seeing. She knelt, trying to get closer to Kerry. Of course it was futile. She was on Earth. He was wherever the golden fields were. Neither Heaven nor Hell, but wherever it was she was not capable of getting there.

The floor went dark, startling Fiona and she fell backwards.

"The Warden from this post has been released," A voice from everywhere said. "You are intruding."

"I... My name is Fiona Phillips. I'm a journalist."

"That's not the only word you'd use to describe yourself, after what you did to the newborn."

Fiona's throat closed up, as her mind light up with the word: Killer. How was it possible this voice knew how she felt?

"You cannot kill me with that. Not with only three bullets. At best, you can ensure that we meet."

"I'm not using it on myself."

"Very good. Tell me what you want."

Without so much as a second thought, she said, "A typewriter. I doubt this place gets power."

"Again, very smart. I look forward to the piece you will write."

"Who are you?"

"You know of my actions. That Warden showed you a sped-up version of Pursuit's construction."

Fiona heard hate in her voice. The voice clearly belonged to a woman. One who, like Fiona, was fed up with things as they are and wanted to see a change.

"You created the spire?"

"I changed what was already there." There was a sense of pride here as if Fiona had asked this woman about her children.

"What is your name?"

"Most call me Dredge. I quite like it."

Fiona found herself fascinated by the voice and the woman it belonged to. She spoke so carefully and Fiona could feel the weight behind what she was saying. Changed, that's the word she chose. "What do you want from me?"

"Easy. I want you to do what you want—to write. Expose Wick's Tavern for all and together we will watch the place finally go out. Nothing lasts forever."

The blackboard dissolved and in its place was a modest wooden desk, complete with cushioned armchair, much like the one she had at home; on the desk a typewriter appeared, beside it a single piece of paper. She approached it and wound the page into the typewriter. As she opened her mouth to ask Dredge for more, another sheet appeared where the other was.

"What happened to Kerry?"

"The newborn is where he belongs."

"That's not an answer."

"You are like me, Fiona, you want to change things. We can start with the Tavern."

"The gun was changed, wasn't it?"

"Indeed. As was Kerry. As will this whole place, but first you have to help me change it."

"Why do you call him a newborn?"

"Things are different now. The Wardens are not needed, though the ones that remain wish to remain relevant. I'm sorry to say the one you met was not honest with you."

"How so?"

"They asked for more power and I gave it to them. Then they turned so many souls dark. I had to do something. The one you met was the one leading the charge."

"That's why the gun looked like it bled shadow, like he did."

"Exactly. He will be found and dealt with. Don't you worry. Any other questions?"

Fiona thought for a moment, Dredge hadn't answered everything and yet she felt satisfied. And at ease. She shook her head.

"Very well. Your weapon of choice awaits you."

Fiona sat down, without saying a word and began typing. She began with her own ideas of the Tavern and the stories she'd heard over the years. Stories of strange sightings of feral children which turned out to be true. Stricat was the word the Warden had used, and so she decided she'd use it too. She'd heard that at different times in history, people had gathered at Wick's to search the woods for whatever it was that lived out there. There was always something living in the cottage, she thought and subsequently wrote in this quick run of notes and ideas. That which lived in the cottage was what the Tavern used to exact its strange judgment.

Fiona looked to the door and watched it meld away within the wall. It didn't matter because she knew already that she was locked in here. What the Tavern didn't know was she was not about to play along with its game. She looked down at the floor and though it was faint, she heard Dredge.

"Research is important. I want you to get this right. The cottage belongs to you."

Ethan, in his death, had given her what she wanted and as a result she would pay him back by making sure the Tavern was stopped. Her home town would be freed, but most of all, she had a companion that wanted what she wanted.

Dredge.

She was the way into the golden fields of the afterlife. First, the Tavern would fall. Then, she promised herself, she'd find the fields and... Ethan.

Departure

The Warden felt renewed, electrified. The lightning came down, freeing him, but the the truth he kept from the woman tormented him. She held the gun, carried it even and didn't seem to be affected at all. Unlike the one she slayed outside the cottage. It didn't make sense. What had he missed?

The word repeated in his mind. Collision. It wasn't supposed to happen. Everyone had agreed it was just a myth or something that was destined in take place in some distant future. This had to be Dredge's doing. He had to do something about what she did to his home, to his people. That awful jagged tower, a mockery of everything the Wardens were. It was more than an insult—a replacement. He hated it. He hated her.

But now it wasn't a fantasy anymore. He could go home, to the place she had left them: The Shadow Labyrinth. Like the cottage, it was a prison, but it was theirs. It wasn't exactly nothing, but the Wardens should have more. They deserved more.

The stone casing around his arm was not as heavy as it looked and yet now that it was gone, he felt a hundred pounds lighter. The Warden flexed his arm and smiled as he made a fist, and felt the familiar tingle. He didn't have enough. Not yet. He cracked his neck and searched for a landmark to find his bearings. He was still in the forest. The trees told a story—one that he helped shape with the rage of first being stuck here. The lightning sent him deep, but not too far from his ticket off Earth.

He trudged through the Connecticut forest to where his failsafe remained. Every step felt lighter and lighter due to the absence of the stone anchor. Within minutes he was near the tree he had marked with the anger and disappointment of being assigned here. He pressed his closed fist into the larger indentation in the tree. Slowly, he leaned around the tree, fist still in the hole, and saw the beady orange eyes of a stricat. His last meal as a resident of Earth. He spit just outside the crude cage.

The tiny creature gripped the bars and stomped its feet, the thing was trying to tell him something. Suddenly, it all made sense. He never saw the bodies of the ones that the police officer had killed. Their shadow energy had transferred to the gun!

The stricat weren't shades, but they had tiny trace amounts of the shadows that provide the Wardens with their abilities. It was suspected that the stricat realm was nearest the shadow realm, and thus they had unlocked some shadow abilities. He had never seen such things while living with them. They were kind to him, once this male had been removed from the rest. Until the strangers invaded their forest.

That police officer—she had called him Kerry—was an agent of Dredge's.

The Warden reached down and grabbed the tiny creature by its throat and with a flick of the wrist, broke its neck resulting in the dimming of the orange light. He siphoned the shadow as its life winked away. He laughed as the shadow crossed through him. It was worth it. He would have his revenge.

The feeling began in his fingers and rode the bones all the way to the elbow, before expanding and exploding up the rest of the way to the shoulder. He rolled his neck, preparing for the change. Slowly the tingle spread across his chest and down his abdomen. It was swallowing him and he couldn't be more thrilled. He would fade beneath the moonlight and travel to where the Wardens were.

He laughed as it tripped across his neck. Until he saw his hands, he had forgotten how disorienting the change was. They were turning a pale black color. As was the rest of him. He braced himself, locking his knees and balling his fists. He was readying for the jolt of pain that would surely be more than any other previous time.

He had never heard of a Warden coming out of retirement. It's true when they say, "*A first time for everything.*" He thought about the young woman, Fiona. She deserved better, but sacrifices had to be made. He would not feel bad. Nothing could change his mind.

The Connecticut forest was fading from view, while in reality, he was fading from it. That is why his arm was encased in stone. It kept him anchored to the cottage, and now with a little shadow from the stricat, he was feeling like his full self again. A Warden is tied to nothing but the shadows.

The Warden blinked and he was inside the labyrinth's foyer, similar to the cottage, it was in two places at once. While the cottage existed within the land of the living while having a foothold in the after, the labyrinth merely had a corner that folded within the living worlds.

He looked at the two guards who stood at either side of the large sliding stone door that had more in common with a barricade. They had the only weapons that could subdue Wardens, obscuras; spinning plates that when thrown unraveled into long pieces of stones that wrapped around like a snake.

The two guards held their hands up, stopping the Warden. They wanted to know why he is back, but no words were spoken. Only meanings conveyed.

They lowered their hands and together they rolled the door aside, allowing him passage. Strolling through the open door exposed the long corridor that began the labyrinth. Along each side of the hall should be filled with his fellow Wardens, but there was no one. Only the echo of what it was like when he was here last and what it should be. It was foolish to think it would be the same. That's why he was forced out. In the room at the center of the labyrinth would be the one who opposed him.

This time it would be different. Much different.

His steps were slow and heavy as he let the reality of being back creep in, not only his mind, but his flesh. He was home. He didn't expect a big welcome, but at the very least he expected a handful of surprised Wardens to rush toward the door. Disappointment was all he found in the silent hallway that began the labyrinth.

The labyrinth was an anomaly. It wasn't a place anyone could happen upon, not like the obsidian spire called Pursuit, which loomed over the fields of the afterlife. The labyrinth was a secret place. The Warden never quite understood the need for guards outside, then again, if he was at full power he could have bypassed them all together and found where his kinfolk were gathered, yet got his surprised reaction.

The lowly stricat was not enough to do that and he thought it'd be fine, but it wasn't. He should have kept two locked up together, however that would have been troublesome. The one he had isolated was to prevent further breeding. That particular stricat was rambunctious and was the reason the two stricat quickly became a lot more.

He felt the tingling sensation leave his body. The withdrawals would be next. He traced his newly freed hand against the walls and the elaborate design etched in the stone slabs. The corridor wound to the right and fell into shadow. It soothed him. As he came around the slight corner, he was the one surprised.

His hand dropped to his side, as the new section of corridor lit with low dancing candle flames came into focus. The floor rose uphill, ever so slightly, and he managed to force himself up the incline enough to verify what he was seeing.

The floor was riddled with bodies. His fellow Wardens.

The first he saw was not bloodied. He imagined this Warden was the first to die. Whoever had done this had snuck up and strangled him. He bent down and touched his brother's neck.

It was still wet with sweat.

Weapons were not allowed in the labyrinth and the Wardens preferred it this way. Violence followed those who held tight to weapons.

He looked across to the end of the corridor and knew that whoever had done this was still here. He rose and walked over and around all his fallen kinfolk. One had their face crushed in while another had their limbs twisted backwards, as if they were pushed down and someone tried to tie a knot with all four extremities. He shook his head and hurried through the corpses, trying to separate them from the people he once knew. They weren't people anymore.

Perhaps his time on Earth did change him. He never thought of him and his fellow Wardens as people before. Rephaim were far from people, but not alien. He didn't like thinking of his heritage much. It wasn't discussed among the Wardens. The unspoken truth was they all agreed that the flood was necessary, though the memory remained painful. He wasn't present then, but there were some that were. Were there any left? Regardless of what lie ahead, at least his kinfolk here would be allowed to rest. Once their untimely deaths were rectified.

The Warden put his hand on the only sister Warden within the hall. Her eyes frozen in place like woman he met in the Connecticut forest. Seemed like years ago, and yet he felt younger than he did in the forest. Existing on Earth is heavy. He couldn't remember the Warden's name that laid before him, but he assumed she'd be grateful for the effort he put in to close her eyes. It's difficult to remember names when you don't use them. Not all were mute like him, but those capable were still kinfolk of few words. Unless the alternative was necessary in the field.

At the end of the corridor, he looked right—a dead end—and then went left. It was much the same in the next corridor. Bodies on top of bodies, some bloodied, some not. All dead. Were all the Wardens killed? Could no one stop the killings?

He walked through the carnage, careful not to pay too much attention to the faces or the feeling of gloom that hung heavier than the shadows. Briskly, he pursued whatever truth may await at the end of the trail of bodies. Corner after corner, he rounded and found nothing but corpses. The heart of the labyrinth was close. He hoped he wasn't too late. He hoped he would find an answer. All this carnage had to be paid for.

He felt a pang of fear as he realized the Wardens would not be able to come back from this. Wardens were Rephaim, and they were extinct. A horrible thought shot through his mind: he may be the last. There was nothing he could do to change that. He could not reproduce. To reproduce with a human would be to create something worse than Nephilim, and Nephilim were lower than stricat. He shuddered at the thought of fathering an abomination.

Humanity was correct at least partially with their idea of a great flood, though a bearded fellow who sat on a cloud was far from accurate. In truth, he did not know what lay beyond the golden fields. Maybe there was a bearded man who danced high up in a city of clouds. No, this was the touch of humanity talking. Their ideas were just that.

The Warden lifted his foot over another of his fallen kinfolk and their eyes were darkened—he knew what caused this. The foolish alliance with the one called Dredge. The creator of the dark spire, Pursuit, that became a beacon for souls in the fields. Nearly removing the need for Wardens, as who needed guidance when there was now a landmark in the fields. The curious part was how none of the other realms have intervened because what Dredge had done was steal all incoming souls for herself and her jagged tower.

If only his kinfolk had listened to him. He was right, but he took no satisfaction in it. She wanted them gone and the deal that was struck resulted in him being retired, was the same one that ended the Wardens.

Dredge's proposal involved giving Wardens full reign on choosing and corrupting souls. They could choose their own souls to darken, thus populating Pursuit, and also giving themselves an endless supply of what they needed to travel between the fields and the labyrinth. She wanted more souls in Pursuit and she definitely wanted the Wardens gone. They couldn't see it and he was railroaded.

He heard voices coming from not too far off. He knew he was at the heart of the labyrinth. He knew it must be his opposition. The one that lead the fight for Dredge's proposal. The foolish bastard had done this.

As he turned the last corner, he saw the opposer drop another Warden and smile.

"Ah, Cottage Dweller, so good of you to stop by. Couldn't have planned it better!"

He had nothing to write with and suddenly, he wished he kept one of those guns for himself. The bastard slaughtered them all. The Warden made two fists and snarled.

"Stricat got your tongue?" The opposer giggled, "Oh, I almost forgot. You need something to write with!" He held a curved knife out. "This should help. Go on."

The Warden closed the gap and looked the opposer in the eye, hatred in his heart boiling over. If he didn't look away, he thought he might rupture a blood vessel behind his eye. As he pulled his glance aside, he glimpsed a smile on the opposer's face.

"You can't commit to anything. They'd be ashamed if they could still feel." The opposer swung the blade around and hid it behind his back. There was a click as it found its home in the secret holster at the small of his back.

The Warden felt the emptiness then. His own back was bare. There was nothing, not even words to defend himself with.

"This is over. You're over. I don't have to stick around and kill you, Cottage Dweller. You're hardly alive. Look around you," He swung his arms outward, "I am your better. I am better than all of you. It would be pitiful watching you die, so I'll leave you here with the dead and let them watch."

The opposer darkened and blinked out of the labyrinth. The Warden looked around, part of him hoping it was a bluff. He knew better. He felt the change in the air. If fog had a stench, it'd be similar to a shadow departure. But it wasn't just the atmosphere, he felt the absence of life. Was he already dead?

The stricat he devoured on Earth barely got him to the labyrinth. He can't follow the bastard who did all of this. Once again, he's trapped and there's nowhere to go. No one will come like the young woman did back on Earth. It's hopeless. What little shadow he had left will leave him soon, unused.

Was this what the bastard wanted all along? To corrupt and then kill our whole line? What was the goal?

He thought of Dredge and a memory broke free. He was there when she pitched the idea. He was there when she made herself appear more beautiful than she had any right being. It was all a lure. She lured the bastard and he destroyed the Wardens for her. Because without the them, she could change the fields the same way she changed Sheol.

She wanted control and more than that—she wanted disruption.

She granted the them more power and made sure it would result in their end.

He looked down at the mess of bodies and saw the dark eyes of a Warden look back at him. The shadow energy still remained.

No—it was too crude. But they were dead and he would be too if he didn't...

He looked at the eyes of one of his kinfolk and could almost hear them give permission. That was all he needed. He closed his eyes and felt the twinge of the shadow. There wasn't much left, but it would be enough to drill into the dead. He aimed his palm at the deceased, the rocked his hand back and forth. The shadow spiraled from his palm and vanished into the chest of the body below the Warden.

He closed his eyes and saw a glimpse of the opposer. There was an offer being made, to join together and rule alongside Dredge. It was bullshit and this dead Warden knew it. Darkness snapped down and sent the head of the Warden from the cottage rocking backward.

He opened his eyes, shadow surrounded him. With a smile, he inhaled all the shadow energy. It disappeared up his nose and through his eyes. The shadow coursed through him, more than he had experienced in one fell swoop. The Wardens carried a lot and this fallen kinfolk was overloaded with shadow. He felt incredible, like he could do anything. His heart raced, and then he thought of the next body that stretched out before him.

If he left now then all the shadow energy still in these bodies would go to waste. It wouldn't last dormant and there was no way to preserve it.

One by one, he repeated the process of shadow-drilling into each of the fallen. Each one shared a memory of the opposer and each time his shadow supply was overloaded. He should have done more to try to convince all of them before Dredge took hold. Most of the fallen were blindsided, as they had grown to love the increased power Dredge supplied.

Dredge opened the floodgates and allowed them to create and darken however many souls they wanted. Some were reluctant at first, but as soon as they saw what happened to him, they quickly fell in line. The Warden in charge, the one that he opposed, grew darker and darker by the day. There were some that knew an end was coming. They were afraid. Every single one of his kinfolk he entered knew it without a doubt that a grisly end was in sight for all of them.

The first that was killed that day loved the one who betrayed them all. It was a strange feeling because he was not prepared when he shadow-slipped and felt it immediately like a hurricane. He felt light and then a new fold of the breeze would take him further. After experiencing this many times before, he knew he was reliving her memory and desperately tried to end it. He could not. She had something to show him, one singular moment that told him everything he needed to know.

The female had been in the next room unbeknownst to the Last Warden, as the betrayer had begun to refer to himself even in the company of others. He was talking to someone and the voice that spoke back was not one that the female knew. Dredge's voice was calm as she spoke of sharing Pursuit with the Last Warden. They would reshape the fields and there was more, but it was far off. He couldn't reach it and then it was gone as his body consumed the last of the shadow energy.

But it was clear enough. Dredge wasn't done changing things. She had changed Sheol into Pursuit and now she had changed the Wardens. She was responsible for all of this. The Warden looked back up the hallway that was now splattered with an obscene amount of gore. This was all her fault. Once Dredge was done with the fields, which direction would she go next?

A sudden shockwave rumbled down his forearm and burst into a black circle in his large palm. When he gazed upon it, it changed revealing the gold fields and a person with their back turned, the young person looked over their right shoulder and the Warden was swallowed by his duty.

As he was taken from the labyrinth into the fields, he focused on the young man's fear. That's what activated the Warden's slip because there was something to act on, a human feeling to use against them as they made their way through the field. Every single person was different. Some needed to conquer something and others like this man needed something to run from. The possibilities, like the fields were endless. And yet, Pursuit remained able to tower over the fields.

The golden grass was tall, nearly up to the young man's hips and the Warden had forgotten how cool the grass and the air were in the field. The atmosphere was pleasant, and he was there to disrupt that for this man. He watched as the man trudged through, using his arms to push through the thick grass. Staring at the man, the Warden made no attempt to hide his presence until the man looked over his shoulder then the Warden vanished in a shadow, leaving behind a cloud of dark smoke.

"Who's there?" The man called out, "Where am I?" He turned in a circle and then realigned, facing the only structure or landmark: Pursuit.

He couldn't figure out why Dredge would want to change the layout of the fields and how it has worked for so long. Everything faced her. What more could she want? He pushed the thoughts aside and slipped back to the fields. His feet thudded on the ground less than three feet from the man, scaring him off his feet.

"Whoa! What the hell are you?" The man tried to hurry to his feet.

The Warden stepped toward the man and he took off, straight toward Pursuit. He wished he could tell the man that there was no escape, no sanctuary there, but he was powerless. He had a job to do and it wasn't nearly important enough to create a new path. The Warden watched the man run for all he was worth and after nearly a minute, he followed, making sure to walk as heavy as possible.

He thought of how he wanted change before and that's what got him the cottage which he was sure the young woman, Fiona, entered and maybe she'll be able to do something good with it, but it was unlikely. As the two quickly approached Pursuit, something occurred to him, if he stopped and refused to hear the call of this hapless soul then another Warden would have to be called. There was only one other that he knew of. He stopped and turned away from Pursuit. His eyes closed, he cleared his mind of the chase and the duty. There was a crackle of lightning and the Warden stood still.

Something thudded nearby and he knew what was happening, even without the man screaming—he would have known.

"Cottage Dweller! Look at me and witness what you could have had!"

He turned around, shadow spilling from his eyes like dark smoke.

"So that's how you did it," His opposer grinned.

His hands turned dark and the tingling feeling crept up from his fingertips.

The opposer gripped the hapless man by the neck, then the Warden saw the change.

"You think I'm the villain, but look at you, you still wear the remains of your kinfolk. Our kinfolk." The opposer spoke as the young hapless man appearance changed to a thick darkness. The dark soul was darker than any he'd seen before. Because it was corrupted, it wasn't a proper change. The opposer released the soul, and it stumbled down to its knees. The soul now gazing up at the Warden, with its bulging black eyes. The darkness was hollowing the soul out unlike the shadow energy, which blended and was in unison with their bodies. Human souls are not meant to be turned this way.

He stared at the opposer.

"This would be easy if you spoke. Oh, that's right, you one of those. A blackboard Warden." He laughed.

The Warden balled his hands into fists, felt his jaw clench. The bastard was taunting him, trying to get him to make the first move, so that he could siphon some of the energy he had built up. Wherever the bastard slipped in from must have been far because he was being overly cautious. The tables were turned, but not for long because as soon as the last of the humanity burst from the soul, then it would be over and the bastard would take everything the soul had; which would be more energy than he had since his energy was stolen second hand.

"You're thinking about how awful it is that I corrupted this poor soul. Thing is, he was destined for this. Things do not happen in the fields unless they are meant to. The humans got that right about their gods. Things happen for a reason. And this man died for this. Dredge confided in me. I have a place in Pursuit. I'm sure I could find one for you as well, if you'd yield."

The Warden looked at the man, his eyes were nearing the end, the final bursting. He remembered the other man, the one in the woods that was turned a more natural way and then it all came into focus. He knew exactly what he had to do.

Releasing his fists, he let the shadow energy form black circles in his palms. All he had to do was keep the asshole talking. He motioned his head toward Pursuit and that was all he needed to do.

"Everything points there. It's where we were meant to go, but you had to disagree and force my hand, and then to make sure there was no one else she had me kill everyone. I'm the Last Warden and you could be my partner. We could be the Last Wardens. Together."

The Warden extended his hand and when the opposer gripped it, the Warden brought his other hand and connected it to the opposer's. Black smoke rose around them, and they vanished, together, from the fields in a swirling shadow.

***

When he opened his eyes, the realm of the stricat did not disappoint. The stench of it was overwhelming, it smelled of dust and sweat. He'd never been before, but he'd heard many stories of it. The darkness around started shifting and echoing chattering filled his ears. They were surrounded.

The opposer jumped backward, "What? What do you think you're doing? They are going to kill us!"

The crowd of stricat moved in, and the Warden saw beyond them to the forest that stretched as far as he could see. It was made up of stiff looking trees that resembled sculptures of trees rather than living things. Further, he saw what he first thought to be mountains were actually tall flames.

He was stunned by the sight of it all.

The cement trees were without leaves, but had the same structure as the winding limbs of the mountain laurel trees he'd seen plenty of in Connecticut. He could imagine the small stricat bounding and running through the trees like children on monkey bars. The mountainous flames were the only light source, and it created an eerie outline through the crowd. Matched with the eerie orange eyes. The Warden was terrified, but he held tight. He could never be as scared as the opposer was. He was hollering and waving his arms, which only attracted the stricat.

The Warden smiled as the eyes of his opposer made their way to him.

"You're enjoying this?" He said, his voice quaking.

He focused his mind on the creation. There was enough shadow to take him back to the fields, but only because it wasn't far from the stricat realm. If he was lucky, then a few stricat would follow him, but the way they were all focused on his opposer, he didn't think it was likely. He felt the shadow form the dark circles in his palms, and he waved wiggling each of his fingers to his opposer as the shadow swallowed him whole, vanishing him from the stricat realm.

As he slipped, he heard the opposer's last words: "This isn't over!"

The cool air of the fields wafted all around the Warden, he looked to Pursuit and he started towards it. There was nothing in his way. Nothing to stop him from getting there and storming the ugly place. She would not change the fields. She wouldn't be able to because there has to be something driving the souls one way or another. The stricat would not work. It had to be a Warden, one way or another.

Afterword

T**hank you for reading.**

I hope you will consider leaving a review! It's something small that you can do that directly impacts my career and the perception of my books.

I look forward to reading what you think of my work.

You've just completed the first book of the ongoing series entitled The Pursuit of Shadows. Books 2 and 3 are finished and are either available very soon or now, depending on when you read this.

I know you have questions, and those questions have answers. Like why was the Warden thinking about Collision? What does that mean? Look for the answer in Book 3!!

These days many things are started and then promptly cancelled before the story is fully realized or completed. This book, The Last Warden, is both an intro and a pledge. **I am going to write 5 books.** Books 1-3 are shorter than a traditional novel, but I expect books 4 and 5 to be more akin to a traditional novel (250 or more pages).

There's a lot of story to tell and I plan to tell it all. I hope you'll go along for the journey with me.

-Edward Kane

January 2025

Preview

Coming May 2025 is Book 2 of

The Pursuit of Shadows

Ruiner

The following is a preview of the first chapter.

Ruiner - Chapter 1

Fiona Phillips pressed the ancient return key and removed the page from the antique typewriter. She glanced it over quickly and placed it where she had placed the last one—and the one before that—directly to her left. As soon as it hit the small wooden desk it vanished, she placed her hand to the right of the typewriter where a fresh sheet appeared. She fed it into the typewriter and continued typing. Fiona was running solely on instinct. Her mind was firmly adrift with the writing and would not allow any other thought inside until the task was done. Until the truth of Wick's Tavern was on the page for any and all to read.

Rendbury put their trust in the Tavern, Fiona knew they didn't need to. It was time for change. She was honored to be the one bringing about this change. The Tavern and it's proprietor were done doing the judging. Now it was her turn.

The next page was done. She placed it to her left while grabbing the next one on the right, wound it into the machine, her fingers began to fill the page once more—typing away. There was no telling how many pages she'd done or how long she'd been inside the strange cottage that once held the Warden prisoner. She figured it was a rotating thing. Once one left, another came in, yet she was different. She was fighting back.

Another page disappeared to the left, as a fresh one appeared on the right. Within moments, it was full of her words, then she repeated the process again.

When she placed the next to her left and reached to the right, nothing was there. She looked around, searching for paper, as she pondered where she ended the previous page. It wasn't completely full of words because she had come to the end of the story. She had done it.

The exposé article on the Tavern was in the world—somehow. Dredge must have some influence elsewhere in the world.

Fiona turned away from the desk and looked at the cottage. The faux glass floor and the blackboard. It was full of tools, and she had used them all. There were frantic scratchings on the blackboard about connections between deaths near the Tavern. Ethan was the most legible of those scratchings because he was the most important of them. He was in the fields, she knew. But what they meant exactly, she wasn't sure. He knew about the Tavern, and yet he still came out here and was devoured by little monsters called stricat. She didn't go into that much detail in her article because one, she was trying to be a respectable journalist. Two, who the hell is going to believe in weird little demon children with orange eyes?

"So I'm done and I'm still stuck in this place?" She said aloud to no one but herself. The door had dissolved into the wall when she first arrived, and she assumed it would return when her job was finished. She didn't want to think about how long she'd be up and writing for. It had been long, she knew because she could feel it, a long with the fog within her mind.

She collapsed onto the bed in the corner of the room. It was hard and bounced way too much. It was all spring, no cushion, and yet she was asleep instantly.

***

"Ethan Brahm and Fiona Phillips," He said, "It's nice. You'll come around, Fiona." Ethan was standing a foot from her and she knew he was right because that goddamn smile was too much.

She'd never be able to withstand it.

"Fine, one date and we'll see how it goes," She surrendered.

Images fluttered all around her like playing cards that displayed fragments of their relationship. Their first date which wasn't much to write home about. So many cards showed them in the car, that gorgeous blue car. She longed for these days. The days in the car. She didn't recall much of what happened around them, just the roads, the car, and the music.

Before they graduated there were plenty of joints, but then they had to get serious and serious they did. Yet the car remained their fortress.

She reached out toward a dark card, helplessly she watch it spin until the other side faced her. It said, "Ending" in bold print and the letter g had a little flare at the end, the way he always wrote them.

Letters and little notes flashed around her, and then she was facing the "Ending" again.

"Fiona, you have to listen to me. Look at me," Anita ordered, "I'm trying to help you."

The words were there but the actual memory was gone. She didn't want to remember it all. She didn't like remembering the ending. Even the words hurt.

"If you stay, this is all you'll ever be. This town is all there'd be for you and Ethan. Fiona Brahm is a dream and you'll never be awake—you'll never be what you want to be. You really think you dropped out of police academy because it's unchanging? Bullshit, Fi. Bullshit." Anita's tough love was still tough even years later.

Fiona didn't reply. There was nothing to say. Anita knew her.

"Fiona, we both know you have aspirations and Ethan will never water those seeds."

He cried when she told him. Fiona knew that in some ways, she was the thing that filled the hole where his mother should be, but that wasn't her fault. She reminded herself, time and time again. She wasn't responsible for that.

Her body twitched and her eyes opened. She had been dreaming. Tears began when she thought of how long she sat crying after breaking up with Ethan and then she fled to college. She wasn't there when his dad died or when he started drinking heavily. Anita made sure she stayed away. Anita worked very hard to drive her away and then was the one that called her back.

She thought of how Anita had changed because of her usage of orbs that a man with a bowling ball bag came to town with. Using the orbs made Anita older, she had given part of herself over in order to use the magic. Fiona shook her head, how had her life become this?

"Did those orbs show her other things?" Fiona wondered aloud, looking at the floor, but it did not show her anything. It stayed the glassy black like a smartphone with a dead battery. It used to respond to her and was invaluable in providing a research channel. Maybe she wasn't meant to know the answers to some questions.

Like what made Ethan go to the Tavern and have his last drinks? It will bother her for the rest of her days, but that was the way of the living. The dead took their answers with them.

She considered asking the floor other questions like how she survived without food or what day it was, or maybe something about Ethan. But she knew it wasn't worth it. Chances were there would be no reply and if there was a change in the floor then it would probably show her something she didn't want to see. She'd done what she set out to do and she hoped that Dredge would do her part by letting her out of this tiny cottage. But there was enough satisfaction from just the work that made her feel okay with the living situation. Nothing was permanent, she told herself, day in and day out.

***

Dreaming and waking, Fiona felt like she was on a seesaw—floating up and sinking down. This time the sinking was the waking. She groaned as her eyes opened. Yelping as her feet hit the cold floor, which reminded her to put her shoes back on before rising and gazing into the black glass of the floor. Fiona wondered if there was a question the window of the floor would answer.

After a stretch, she stood and walked to the center of the room. Looking up and then down, Fiona cleared her throat and asked the floor, "If I were to ask you something about... Ethan Brahm, would you answer truthfully?" After a moment, "I want to trust you."

She didn't move. Her eyes fixed on the floor like she was willing it to answer. Fiona curled her hands into fists and felt the twinge of pain as her nails dug into her palms. No blood, only pain. Off in the corner, something danced along the floor. She darted her eyes toward it and saw a blossoming of smoke. An image was coming through. Dark purple smoke rolled and expanded, giving way to a message in elegant cursive handwriting.

"I've always been honest with you, Fiona."

"That's not an answer."

"Ask your question," the floor message read.

This was personal and she wasn't sure if she should share her most personal ideas with whoever was on the other side of this thing, but what else was there to do? She nodded and asked her question.

"Can you show me where he is?" She knew he had to be in the fields. From what little she knew of the afterlife, she knew he had to be having a rough time of it.

The smoke below her vanished, leaving only a dark spot. She squinted at it, unsure what to make of what she was seeing and then he turned around.

Ethan. She was looking right at Ethan. His face took up most of the floor, it was all she could see. The view was zoomed in too much because the entity on the other end did not want Fiona seeing what was around Ethan. His eyes were large. He was afraid. Fiona's stomach jumped in pain and her heart was pounding. Here he was, and she'd give just about anything to talk to him, but it wasn't possible. He was dead. She was in this strange purgatory.

She wanted to scream. His hair was the same black wavy mess that she adored. His eyes were the color of a summer sky. Everything was as it was, and yet it wasn't. They were farther apart than two people had ever been before. There was no way for her to fix any of it. No way to turn back time. It didn't matter why he went to the Tavern. What mattered was he was in the fields. The golden fields that were patrolled by giants who called themselves Wardens. It was only a matter of time, one would be coming for him.

Was there a way for her to help?

She stared at the face of the only man she had ever loved. It seemed so long ago now, like it happened to someone else. But she could still feel the fluttering in her chest and her stomach just from looking at his face. All those nights sitting beside him in the car, his hand holding hers. Those moments were everything and she gave it up. She decided to pursue something greater than herself because he had no aspirations? No, Anita convinced her because he had no future, but how could she know that? Anita said she was worried about Ethan corrupting her dreams. What did that mean exactly? Was choosing love so wrong?

Fiona groaned at herself. "I need to get the fuck out of here or I'm going to drive myself crazy."

She trusted her friend's advice. Maybe it was crazy, maybe it wasn't. She couldn't change it now.

This tiny room was messing with her. She closed her eyes and tried to let everything fade from her mind. Such an easy thought, but she wanted to feel like she was in control of something. Again, she turned away from Ethan and walked to the wall where the door was, reaching out slowly she touched where the knob should be. She heard the click in her mind as she turned her hand. Fiona yanked and did her best to imagine the door opening, it was no use. She pulled and nothing happened. She mimed the turn again and yanked even harder. Her ass collided with the floor. She cursed.

"What is the point of any of this? Why am I here?" She called out toward the ceiling while gripping her hand. The throbbing pulsed up her forearm and she let out a scream that she'd been holding in since she heard the news of Ethan's passing.

She didn't want to leave, and she definitely didn't want to turn around to look at him. She just wanted it all to be over. How much could she take? Maybe she should have run away with Anita when she offered the night she came out here and met the Warden. She remembered what Dredge had said when she had entered the cottage: "You are like me, Fiona, you want to change things. We can start with the Tavern."

Fiona uncurled herself from the ball she'd rolled herself into. She made no effort to wipe the tears away, as she stood she said, "Are you there?"

At first there was nothing, but then she heard something almost like a creaking door. Perhaps there was a window peering into the cottage as well as many other places. Surely the person that sits at the top of the sole structure in the afterlife would have many places to look in on.

"Yes, dear, someone is always here."

"Why are you keeping me here? When we could be changing things together?"

"Are you certain that's what you want, Fiona?" Dredge's voice sounded eager.

"Yes. Now tell me why you're keeping me here."

"I had thought you would need more convincing."

"Convincing... of what?"

"These two buildings, the cottage and the Tavern work in unison. The stories you've heard are true, for the most part. On a larger level, the conversation between the two structures is a warning system."

"What kind of warning?"

"Earth is kept at a very long arm's reach from the rest of the realms. While there are always intersections, like the stricat, those pesky bastards multiply without a thought, things usually play by the rules. Until..." Dredge didn't finish the thought.

"The gun I found. Kerry's service weapon. It scares you?"

"Precisely. I thought maybe we need to keep the Tavern where it is, in case your town decides to foster more... *trouble.*"

"What do you want from me?"

"If you are serious about changing things, then—"

"Yes!" Fiona blurted out, interrupting Dredge.

"You want me to push harder?"

"Push what?"

"I can push and see if we can get the Tavern to respond to what you wrote. Or rather, the people to respond. It's the Tavern that will be at the receiving end."

"If it gets me out of here, yes. Do it. Now." Desperation bubbled up her throat, lacing every sound she made.

There was a pop, then silence. Fiona was all alone, again.

***

To be continued...

in

The Pursuit of Shadows

Ruiner

www.ingramcontent.com/pod-product-compliance
Lightning Source LLC
Chambersburg PA
CBHW030434120726
47903CB00003B/961